A ROYAL ROMANCE

CINDY REDDING

CHAPTER 1

*E*mma Louise Harris sat in one of the twelve high-back leather chairs at the mahogany conference table on the eighty-fifth floor of Collins and Collins Architectural Design Firm. Morning sunlight streamed into the room, and the floor-to-ceiling windows along two walls framed the view of the Hudson River and New York Harbor. Ferries and other vessels dotted the waterway. At the head of the table, her boss, the elder Collins and founder of the multi-billion-dollar company, sat in a dark-navy, pinstriped, three-piece suit, white silk shirt, and gold cufflinks with a matching tie pin.

Mr. Collins addressed the group. "His Majesty, the King of Malagra, hired our firm to design a new state-of-the-art hospital in the capital city of Santini. You each have a file with the details and our timeframe."

Emma reached for the folder, flipped it open, and looked at the cover photo. She gasped. The sapphire-blue eyes that stared back at her sent a hum of excitement up her spine. His familiar gaze was all she could think about. She admired the chiseled features of his dark, handsome face. His raven-black hair. They had shared three wonderful days and nights together, stranded in Rome, at the Grand Medici Hotel. Studying his photo, her heart thumped faster as she thought back to when she had first met him. If it weren't for the volcano that erupted spreading ash across Europe their paths would never have crossed.

Not many people had been in the lobby of the hotel at that time of day as they were out having lunch or sightseeing. She'd surprised herself at how quickly she had fallen into his bed. It wasn't his extreme height or his very good looks that first attracted her to him. No, it was the subtle, seductive scent of his cologne. The hot and spicy woody notes had wafted around her and she'd slowed her step. "Pardon me. Are you the hotel manager?"

"Sorry, I am not… although I wish I were just so I could assist you," he'd said in the dreamiest Italian accent she'd ever heard.

"Me too," she'd whispered. "Will you be my knight in shining armor?"

His piercing blue eyes had flared. "I can be whatever you want." A slow grin spread across his sensuous lips, mesmerizing her before he'd drawled, "Actually, I left my armor at the palace."

Emma had laughed at his joke. "I was going to have lunch before I made my way to the airport."

He'd leaned down from his height, and his spicy, sexy scent enveloped her. His low, husky voice rumbled through around her. "Haven't you heard? The airports throughout Europe are closed. All flights are grounded until further notice."

"Yes, and sadly, there is no room at the inn. I'm destined to sleep on the airport floor." Six other men in black suits that were almost as impeccable as his, had silently stepped away, leaving the two of them alone in the semi-empty lobby. "Perhaps I can be of assistance after all."

She'd stretched her neck to look up at him. "Unless you know the hotel manager, I don't think so. I'd already checked out of my room to catch my flight, and then I received a text that it was cancelled."

"Yes, the ash from the volcano that erupted the other day is causing havoc across Europe. You said you were going to have lunch before you go to the airport. Will you join me in the restaurant?"

Emma had never felt such a strong attraction to a man before. She couldn't stop herself from saying yes. "I would like that very much."

From the grand marble and granite lobby, they'd gone up the steps of the open spiral staircase to the three-Michelin-star restaurant.

He had a dimple in his chin, and his upper lip made a perfect bow to his full lower lip. During lunch, she'd caught herself wondering how his sculpted lips would feel kissing her. How would that dreamy mouth feel moving down her body? He had long fingers and an olive complexion with thick, black hair. The blue tie around his neck, over his silk blue shirt, was an exact match for his eye color. How would he look naked? She had to stop herself from imagining it. She couldn't stop herself. Emma tapped the folder on the conference table. The time they had spent together was like a dream.

He'd been honest with her. While sitting at a secluded table in the restaurant, they made plans to make the best of the time they had together while they were grounded. The remainder of their seafood risotto had been removed and they'd lingered over their wine.

His sapphire-blue eyes had held her gaze. "I'm thirty-four and healthy—"

"Oh, is that code for..." She'd lowered her lashes for a moment.

He'd flashed a bone-melting smile at her. "What do you think?" His sexy voice had vibrated into her core.

"Then I'm healthy too. You may continue," she'd said as she leaned back in her chair and taken another sip of wine. Gratefully, her hand hadn't trembled as excitement sizzled through her.

His bow-shaped lips quirked, and a flame ignited in the deep-blue depths of his gaze before he'd said, "I'm not married or in a relationship. Now, it's your turn." One dark brow hinted at rising.

She'd grinned. "I'm twenty-eight, single, and definitely not in a relationship." She'd leaned across the white damask-covered table and whispered, "I would prefer not filling up on dessert."

His dazzling smile widened to show his perfect white teeth, and the corners of his eyes crinkled. "Are you a mind reader? I would rather we had dessert... in my suite... much, much later." He'd meshed his long fingers with hers, kissing her hand before they'd left the restaurant.

"My carry-on is at the bell desk."

He'd leaned down, and his warm breath tickled her ear. "You want to put on more clothes?"

"No," Emma had eagerly replied.

"We'll send for your luggage later."

He had rested his hand on the small of her back, and they'd walked over to a bank of elevators. He'd removed a brass key from his jacket pocket. Inserting the key into a slot, the elevator doors silently opened.

As the doors closed, he'd said, "I can give you this time here and now. It is all I can share with you. I cannot give you tomorrow."

She'd pressed her finger over his gorgeous lips. "It will have to be enough."

Then he'd gathered her into his powerful arms.

"I know we agreed to no names, but now, I want to know. At least tell me your first name."

"Massimo—my name is Massimo."

"I'm Emma Harris."

"Miss Harris," Mr. Collins said.

She looked up, startled out of her memories. "Yes, sir."

"I want you to take charge of the preliminary groundwork for this project. I know you have just returned from leave… but you have the previous experience necessary for this. Can you do that?"

"Of course, sir."

"Good, then put your team together. You leave in a week."

Emma gathered the file as the meeting ended. John Smith, the lead architect on the project, stopped her. "We missed you, and I'm glad you're at least doing the prelims for this project. You really are the best."

"Thanks, John. I'll look everything over and get back to you if I have questions." Emma hugged the file to her breasts as she left the conference room and hurried down the hall. In the privacy of her own office, she ran her finger over his photo, tracing his lips. *He's a king?* A year had passed. 365 days since those three wonderful days and nights. The curve of his smile took her back to… Rome.

The man who led her off of the private elevator and into the living room of the presidential suite was tall, with broad shoulders and a narrow waist. His expensive suit accented his great build. It was early afternoon, and the green velvet drapes were drawn wide to show off the panoramic view of the Eternal City. The dome of Saint Peter's Basilica stood out in the distance against a cloudless blue sky.

"Oh, my, this is so much better than the airport floor I was planning to spend the night on."

Massimo tugged her into him. His lips brushed her hair. "We have to make enough memories to sustain me for a lifetime," he said.

She looped her arms around his neck. "Don't talk, just kiss me... make love to me."

Mid-morning of the third day, they were lying on the rumpled sheets of the enormous bed in the luxurious presidential suite when the phone rang. Sorrow flooded her then. She knew it was over.

Massimo rolled away from her, onto his side to reach for the phone, and the sculpted muscles of his broad back shifted under his olive skin. Heat flushed her cheeks. Massimo had three long, red welts on both sides of his torso and more crescent-shaped marks along his shoulders. She'd never left scratches on a man's back before. Emma had dug her nails into him at the height of their passion—when he was deep in her, more than her one previous lover had ever been—she'd screamed in pleasure. Another thing she'd never done in her very limited experience with the only other man she'd gone to bed with.

Only with Massimo did she scream or have multiple orgasms. She'd thought that was a myth until Massimo proved it not only was possible, but it happened every time.

"I see," he said into the phone before dropping the receiver back on its cradle. When he turned to her, his lips compressed in a grim line as the corners turned down. He combed his fingers through his thick, raven-black hair. "The airport will reopen in two hours, and my flight was called."

Emma heard the sadness in his deep voice and echoed his words, "I see."

He dragged her naked body onto his lap, his long fingers combing her hair from her face.

"Please don't do this. I never offered you what I cannot give."

She shrugged her shoulder. "I know... I thought... it wouldn't hurt—"

His sleep-warm lips smashed onto hers, opening her mouth to slide his tongue in. Could she memorize him?

"I'll always remember you and this time we shared," he whispered against her brow. Then he rolled her under him, and time stood still for a while. She wanted him to stay buried deep in her forever. Her heart ached.

Once they dressed, he said, "I've arranged for you to stay here until your flight is called. I was told that it may be later today or tomorrow as the airports work at getting the planes back into the air. A car will take you to the airport."

Massimo removed the round medallion he wore on a gold chain and put it on her. The medallion, warm from his body heat, rested between her breasts. Her eyes stung, holding back tears. The muscles in her throat constricted and moved as she tried to compose herself.

"I'll never forget you." He pressed his forehead to hers. "Emma, you are the woman of my heart."

"Please go now," she said. "Don't look back. Please, just go." Her voice was full of unshed tears.

She heard the groan from deep in his chest as he enfolded her into his strong, powerful body. He held her in an all-consuming embrace, his lips devouring hers before he stepped back.

Massimo kissed her brow one last time, then did as she'd asked, silently closing the door behind him.

She was too numb to do more than tell herself to breathe. His scent lingered in the air as a tear slid down her cheek, then another and another. She crumpled onto the thick Persian rug of the luxurious presidential suite. For how long she lay there, she didn't know. It was gloomy outside, and she thought how appropriate to match her feelings. The hotel phone rang, startling her. "Hello."

"Miss Harris, this is the concierge. Your flight will depart at six

this evening. I will have a car waiting to transport you to the airport at four. Do you need a bellman for your bags?"

"No, thank you. I only have my carry-on." She hung up the phone and went to splash cold water on her face.

She would forget him—she could do it. When she arrived home, she searched on the internet for the symbols inscribed under the lion on the medallion. Even though the internet was a plethora of information, she never found the answer she was looking for.

Now, all this time—365 days—later, Emma searched on the royal website of Malagra and fingered the medallion that never left her neck; well, except once, when she was in the delivery room, having his son. He was born with thick, wavy black hair, just like his father.

Emma typed King Massimo of Malagra on her keyboard and photos of him appeared on her screen. One was of him in uniform, with gold cord epaulets at his broad shoulders, a blue sash across, hanging at his narrow waist. Medals and decorations covered his left chest. On his hip, a sword in an ornate scabbard. The caption read *His Majesty, the King.*

The official portrait hung in public buildings throughout the kingdom of Malagra. Then there was one of him in a tuxedo, smiling, and another with his crown and robe on. He sat on a red velvet and gold throne. That caption read simply, *The throne room at Santino Palace, His Majesty King Massimo's coronation.*

Her breath caught. *Was he married? Did he have children?* She scrolled through an article. Relief flooded her. He was single. *What would he say if he knew we made a baby?* She had to see him. Tell him about their son.

Would he be at the meeting in Malagra? No, probably not. This was only the prelim. Emma would check out the site, make sure it would work, meet with Prince Gino, the Minister of Urban Development, go over all the tests, order more if necessary, then prepare her mockup based on the architect's design, etc.

Emma leaned against the back of her desk chair as she rubbed her thumb and finger over the thick gold rope chain. She tilted her head and sighed. Her fingers closed over the symbol she wore around her neck. It was part of the king's royal crest. Then the words that she'd never been able to decipher until seeing them now. *I serve with honor and duty.*

On the official website of the Kingdom of Malagra, she found an article entitled, *The Kings of Malagra.* She read about how Massimo's great-great-great-grandfather had held his son's lover captive prior to having her banished from the kingdom, even though he'd been a crown prince. The king had waited to take the child she'd carried from her. The baby belongs to Malagra, he'd stated in the article. She did not.

No longer elated and not sure if she should tell Massimo about her son, Emma became concerned. All at once, his words made sense to her. "I'm Massimo, only Massimo; this is all I can give you." They'd never talked about their lives beyond Rome. She didn't know what to think.

The thud of her heart increased as panic gripped her. She glanced at the photo of Steven that she kept on her desk. Would Massimo be happy about her news? Would he take her baby from her? Apparently, he could. Steven Max Harris, her son, did resemble his father. He was born with a head full of black hair, and his eyes were the exact sapphire blue as his father's. She clicked out of the website as icy fear consumed her.

CHAPTER 2

King Massimo Stephano Luca Giovanni of the House of Santino sat in the back seat of his silver Rolls Royce. The Mediterranean Sea glistened in the distance below, with the capital city spread out from the sea to the foothills of Monte Santino on this bright and clear spring morning.

His driver navigated the palm and cypress tree-lined road that wound from the palace to the main gate and into the heart of the city of Santino. Massimo was on his way to the offices of his cousin Prince Gino, the Minister of Urban Development. The privacy screen was raised, and his trusted personal aide and friend, Nicolo Rana, sat beside him. The head of the royal guard rode in the front seat next to the driver. Two police officers on motorcycles, lights flashing, led the way, and an SUV with six more guards followed.

"What's on the agenda after this?" he asked Nicolo.

"Lunch with your mother, sir. Just the two of you."

He sighed. "In that case, I'm sure the subject of my lack of a queen and heir will come up."

"She seems quite determined, Your Majesty."

Massimo nodded. He should have been married by now. Actually, well before he became king would have been ideal. It was unfortunate that his father died nine years ago. At twenty-five, Massimo had to take charge and lead the nation through a period of sadness. After that, the global economic downturn took all of his skill and time in his efforts to keep Malagra prosperous and a player on the world stage.

"I know that I must marry soon and produce an heir or two; I don't need more pressure from my mother."

"Yes, Your Majesty. The people would love to hear of an engagement, and the prime minister would be delighted to announce your marriage."

Massimo peered out the window and waved to the crowds lining the street.

He had sex—a basic biological need—but nothing more than that. Massimo put serious relationships on the back burner. No long-lasting commitments for him. Most women, he'd learned through the years, couldn't see past his royal title. They were too busy trying to impress and become his queen to notice him, the man. Still, with all of that, Massimo would have married by now, except for one thing.

His biggest problem was that since last year and his unscheduled layover in Rome, he measured every woman against Emma. Those three days and nights with her kept playing over and over in his mind. He couldn't stop himself. His reaction to her had been instantaneous—some people would call it a thunderbolt. Whatever name you gave it, he couldn't think of kissing another woman; undressing someone else became a chore.

A year later, he had to stop thinking of the petite beauty and her ravishing body or her quick wit. He had to do what was right for his country and his people—marry a woman of royal blood and produce an heir. It was his duty, and

Massimo resigned himself to that. He was prepared to do what he must. No more delaying the inevitable.

They drove past the site of the new hospital. The group of architects and engineers from Collins and Collins' New York office were finishing their preliminary work. Once the site received the green light, he would hold a news conference and make the official announcement to the people of Malagra.

Soon after that, he would have to announce his engagement. He decided to marry Lady Luisa. His only concern was that she was young, just twenty-five. Luisa ticked off all the boxes: intelligence, beauty, and her royal bloodline being the most important criteria. She had been vetted, they discussed the marriage and Luisa had agreed. So, he would do what he must and marry her. *Too bad the perfect woman for me isn't possible. Don't I have a right to some happiness?*

Emma slipped back into his thoughts. Not a day went by that he hadn't thought of her. Her beauty was classic, with curves that would send Venus into hiding. Emma was funny and quick with her witty comebacks. She had the sexiest laugh; he could still hear it in the recesses of his mind. On the second day at the hotel in Rome during the afternoon, she'd taken one of his shirts and rolled the sleeves up above her delicate wrists. She was barefoot, and her lustrous red hair cascaded around her. A smile touched his lips as he remembered how she'd called him Maxy.

Emma had downloaded an app on her phone, and they'd played games. Trivia was fun, but she'd accused him of having too many holes in his general knowledge of everything stupid. Why didn't he know what was the best takeout food?

"Oh, you mean take away," he'd said.

Her brows had furrowed. "Yes, okay, take away."

"I don't... do that," he'd said.

She'd shrugged. "Oh well. Next question. Who's your favorite band? Maxy, you must have one."

He'd hummed a tune, then she sang the words. He'd joined her as they sang together. Massimo had drummed his hands on his thighs, and she'd clapped to the tune. He could be himself with Emma. He'd liked that about her. When he thought of Emma's response to his lovemaking, heat rose into his groin. Seated in the car, he fought the urge to close his eyes and relive each erotic moment of his time in Rome. Sex was what he'd had before Emma. No woman had ever shown him the passion she had, taking him to heights he'd never reached before. Emma was everything he could ever want in a woman, a wife, and the mother of his children.

A large crowd had gathered behind the metal barriers along the tree-lined cobblestone street. Massimo waved to the men and women who came to see him as they drove down the street. His car stopped at the majestic former palazzo built in the eighteenth century by one of his ancestors. The building now housed the Office of Urban Development.

Massimo slowly took in a breath. His security team was stationed along the way. Men and women stood on either side of the red carpet, eager for him to exit the car. Gino waited near the curb. One of his royal guards opened Massimo's door, and he stepped out, fastening the button on his charcoal-gray, custom-made suit. Except for that time in Rome when Nicolo and the head of the royal guard advised against it, he always wore his signet ring on his left pinky. Today, he'd added a tie pin with his monogram and his favorite solid-gold wristwatch. It had been a gift from his parents for his eighteenth birthday when he was officially given the title, His Royal Highness, The Crown Prince. At the ceremony, he'd sworn his allegiance to Malagra and signed the official documents proclaiming him heir to the throne of

Malagra and binding him to marry a woman with royal blood.

The breeze from the Mediterranean, with its briny undertone and the fragrance of roses blooming around the baroque building, scented the air.

His cousin Gino was ten years older than him, several inches shorter, with brown hair and a huge, friendly smile. He bowed his head. "Your Majesty, it is an honor to welcome you to the ministry today."

Massimo shook his hand. "I understand you're ahead of schedule."

"Yes, and the team from Collins and Collins will depart for New York tomorrow."

"Well then, it's a good thing I could squeeze your invitation into my schedule."

"Yes, sir. Very good. I think you will be happy with the design."

Massimo waved to those who lined the way into the building. The crowd cheered, and many raised their phones to take a picture of him. Mothers held their babies up for him to see.

Massimo shook hands with some of the people waiting to greet him on the way into the building. The women curtsied, and the men bowed their heads. He stopped near the entry and chatted with several, even posing for a few selfies.

Gino said, "Sir, the associates from New York are waiting in the main salon. We have a mockup of the design on display for you."

Massimo strolled into the cool building. His eyes adjusted to the light. The lobby in and of itself was magnificent, with marble and granite floors. Larger than life portraits—including an official portrait of him—hung on the central wall between the twin staircases that led to the second floor. They walked into the salon.

His cousin said, "Your Majesty, I would like you to meet the lead engineer on the project, Miss Emma Harris."

Massimo stared in astonishment. His heartbeat almost stopped before it thumped wildly in his chest.

The petite redhead curtsied to him, saying, "Your Majesty," in her sexy, wispy voice.

He extended his hand. "Miss Harris, so nice to meet you."

Her green-eyed gaze met his. He didn't think too long about how her hand felt in his. That led him to think of other parts of her body, like the feel of her breasts when he'd cupped them. He moved on to the next person in line.

Massimo had no idea whose hand he shook or what exactly he said. He went down the line in a haze as surprise gradually turned to anger. *How long has she been here? Why didn't she contact me? She has to know who I am. My portrait is hung in the lobby and all over the country.*

Gino's voice broke into his thoughts. "Sir, would you like to see the mockup? Miss Harris can answer any questions you may have."

Oh, yes, I have questions. Many questions. Why would she hide her presence from me? Massimo kept his anger in check, simmering just below the surface.

"Proceed, Miss Harris," he said in a chilled voice.

Her flaming locks framed her beautiful face. Massimo remembered how her lustrous hair fanned over the pillow in copper waves when he was deep in her heated body or how her hair tented over his abdomen before he brushed the lush strands away from her face—he stopped that thought.

Emma wore a navy-blue jacket and matching pencil skirt with a gray silk blouse and gray high heels. The top of her head just about reached his shoulder. She exuded profession- alism as she answered his inquiries.

He thought of her petite, naked form in his arms. He remembered how wild and abandoned she could be. When he'd lifted her over his shoulder and ran from the terrace to drop her on the bed, her musical laugh floated around him… the way she giggled when he'd tickled her before everything got serious and she'd straddled him. He'd come so gloriously and in an instant, he'd gotten hard again before he rolled her sensuous body under him.

Massimo glanced at her. The slight flush on her cheeks added depth to her green eyes. "This is the architect's vision," she said, "based on the specifications that were given to him. He's incorporated a modern aesthetic that blends nicely with the old-world charm of Malagra."

"Have you traveled through the country?" He breathed in her jasmine scent.

"No. I'm sorry to say, I have not."

Massimo saw the flutter of her pulse at her throat. "A pity. Malagra is as ancient as some of the other cities throughout Europe. Take Rome, for instance." He heard her sharp intake of breath as she turned her head. The arch of her brow rose, and her emerald eyes rounded.

The quiver in her voice surprised him as she said, "The architect studied the landscape, then drew the overall design to incorporate the ancient with the modern. Each of his team members designed specific areas for functionality and work-flow." She moved away from him, putting the fifteen-foot-long table between them. Emma gestured to a smaller design. "Take this, for example. It's a mockup of the operating room. There will be six of them. Along this side of the display, we have a model for each of the major areas of the hospital."

Massimo walked around the table and stopped at her side. He nodded and lifted one brow. "And you, Miss Harris, what do you do?"

She peered at him through her long, dark lashes before she raised her head. He caught the flash of emerald fire in her gaze. "Along with my team of engineers, it is my responsibility to ensure the building can withstand any hazards or forces of nature."

Hazards, forces of nature—indeed. She was a force of nature. She'd grown more beautiful, if that was possible. He hadn't contacted her in the past year, knowing full well he could never give her the life she deserved. He wanted to take her in his arms, crush her to him, and never let her go. Instead, Massimo said, "Thank you for your thorough explanation. Good day to you all."

He turned and walked out of the building. "Thank you for the tour," he said to his cousin, shaking Gino's hand.

He waved to the crowd once more before slipping into the back seat of his car. Nicolo joined him, getting in on the other side. His security team gave the signal to his driver that all was clear.

He turned to Nicolo. "You recognized her?"

"Yes, sir. Rome."

"Did you know she was here?"

"No, I did not."

"Cancel lunch. I'm going back to the palace."

CHAPTER 3

*E*mma held the crisp white note card emblazoned with a crown and, below it, in bold block initials, an M, the Roman numeral two, and an R. Rex Latin for king. Her fingers felt stiff, and the knot in her throat tightened. The butterflies in her tummy swarmed out of control. It was so unlike her to be nervous, but the handwritten note simply said, *Come to my residence at the palace.* He'd signed it, M. No please or thank you, only a command from the King of Malagra and not Maxy, the man she'd fallen in love with when they'd spent three glorious days and nights together in Rome.

Sitting on the soft leather of the limousine's back seat, Emma fidgeted, pulling the hem of her dress down. When the note was delivered earlier, she'd changed into a casual, lightweight green dress with a matching blazer and slipped her phone into her designer crossbody purse. She glanced out the window as the car drove up a winding road. The tree-lined drive, with its manicured lawns, led to elaborate wrought-iron gates. A gold crown sat above, and the king's coat of arms hung in the center on both sides of the gate.

The gate swung open, and the driver continued toward the palace. Her heart thumped in her chest as the white stone structure stretched out before her. *OMG, this is where he lives?* The driver turned the car into a cobblestone courtyard and stopped at an arched portico. Four massive carved marble columns held the roof up.

Two guards in red and white uniforms with shiny gold buttons and black leather knee-high boots stood at attention on either side of the entrance doors. Another guard, also dressed in red and white, the colors of Malagra, opened Emma's car door. She slid out, standing on shaky legs. A man in a black suit approached. He looked to be in his mid-thirties, clean-shaven, and almost as tall as Massimo. "Miss Harris, I'm Nicolo Rana, His Majesty's chief aide. Please, if you will follow me. His Majesty is waiting for you."

Emma breathed deeply as her teeth tugged at the corner of her bottom lip. She stepped into the entry. Two suits of armor, complete with helmets and very menacing long poles with an axe blade and spike on them, stood at attention on either side of the carved wooden doors. She took another deep breath and let it out slowly, trying for calm. The floor of mosaic tiles was a work of art, and dotted throughout the area were sculpted marble statues of Roman gods and goddesses. Between the statues, paintings of castles and landscapes were on the wall. Under the paintings, vases of fresh flowers had been placed on narrow gilt tables.

She was led up a white marble staircase with thick red carpet down the center and further down a hall as wide as a two-lane highway. Portraits of men and women wearing crowns and their coronation robes, some with golden orbs and scepters, lined both sides of the high arched white-and-gold walls.

At the end of the corridor, in front of the white and gilt double doors, two guards stood at attention. As they approached, the guards stepped to the side, and each grabbed a gold knob, opening both doors. Emma's mouth was dry. She ignored the overwhelming urge to run her clammy hands down her dress.

She'd almost made it back home without seeing Massimo. This morning had been stressful enough, getting the project complete. When the minister, Prince Gino, had come into her office, excited that the king was on his way to see them, he'd asked, "Miss Harris, do you know how to curtsy when you meet His Majesty, the King?" She hadn't been at all thrilled by the supposed honor, but rather, had wanted to run.

"Miss Harris, I'll leave you now," Nicolo said, bringing her back to the present.

Massimo stood tall and elegant in the middle of the room. Emma studied him from his broad shoulders to his narrow waist and long, muscular legs; his deep-blue vest and pants matched his eyes. A white silk shirt was open at the neck. For the first time, she questioned her judgement. Why hadn't she ever noticed how regally he'd always carried himself?

She stepped into a massive living room. The room was beautiful in shades of blue and gold. Twin ice-blue watered silk couches on gilt frames faced each other. A marble-topped coffee table on a gold frame separated the couches and on one side of the couch, an end table held a vase full of fragrant pink roses. Drapes in the same ice-blue silk and trimmed with gold fringe covered floor-to-ceiling windows.

"Hello, Emma. Why is it I am the only one who is surprised to see you?" His darkly handsome face settled into a frown.

Emma shrugged a shoulder at him. "You didn't look surprised to see me...as a matter of fact, you looked angry. I will admit that I had time to prepare before I came to Mala-gra. Your photo was in the file I was given on the project.

Besides all of that, your portrait hangs at the government building and the airport. Even Malagran money has your face on it, so I knew who you were." *Not the man I fell in love with.*

"Tsk, tsk, Emma. You were going to leave Malagra without saying hello to me after all we shared?"

"Yes, I was. I saw no reason to bring up the past. I remember your words, 'I can't give you tomorrow.'" Her voice broke. "It makes perfect sense. I've heard rumors of your imminent engagement—is she now the woman of your heart?"

Massimo took a step closer to her and stretched out his palms. "She is not of my choosing," he said in a flat voice. "I must marry someone with a royal bloodline. It is the law of my country. And a Malagran citizen is a bonus. My people are expecting a wedding, and I have to provide an heir." He took two more steps closer to her. In his husky accented voice, he said, "I am bound by my oath..." He closed the space between them with another step, and his sexy, spicy scent assailed her. "Enough about all of that business. Have you eaten?" His blue gaze traveled the length of her.

Keeping her feet planted on the blue Persian rug, Emma fought not to move away from him. "No, thank you, *Your Majesty.* I'm not hungry. If this is all you wanted from me, then I need to go, *Your Majesty.*"

"Come sit with me." He sounded so matter of fact to her. As if a year hadn't gone by and—worst of all—that he would soon be married to another woman. Massimo would take his wife in his arms, make love with her. She would be the one to touch him, feel his hardness thrusting deep. He would give her children. Now, finally, she understood that it could never be. *I made the right decision not to bring Steven and his nanny with me to Malagra. I'll never tell him I had his son.*

Her chest ached as she opened the flap on her crossbody

and reached in. Her fingers closed over the cold metal of the medallion he'd given her.

"I did bring you something... Your Majesty. You can consider it a wedding gift."

She stretched her hand toward him, opening her fist to reveal the gold medallion on its heavy rope chain.

"Here, take this back. I don't believe you or what you said to me that day." Emma was upset at the way her chin trembled, and her lower lip pouted, completely ruining her defiant stance.

He grunted before his head jerked back as if he'd been slapped. Massimo shook his thick mane of black hair and wouldn't accept it. The golden flecks in his blue eyes lit with sparks of fury, and the muscles in his jaw popped.

Emma didn't care. She stalked over to the coffee table in the enormous room and placed the solid-gold medallion on the polished marble surface. Straightening, she turned to face him. Taking a breath to calm herself, she said, "I signed off on the project before I was summoned here. I have approved the site. The job I was sent here to do is finished. My flight is in the morning," her voice broke, "and you won't ever have to see me again."

"Emma..." His voice was a sensuous caress, and the harsh angry lines on his handsome face disappeared. "I don't want to hurt you in any way. You must believe me." He covered his heart with his hand. "I meant it when I said you are the woman of my heart."

Her body tensed. "No. Don't talk to me." A sense of loss settled over her. "Nothing... you say... can make me feel better." A tear rolled down her cheek. She was furious with herself, never wanting him to see her sadness or how vulnerable she was.

He took the few steps necessary to close the distance between them and tugged her into the circle of his arms.

"How about this?" he rasped, dragging her against his powerful, hard frame. His warm, sensuous lips found hers. All reason fled, and the madness of wanting him took over. Her pulse raced, and desire for Massimo flooded her. *Just once more, and I'll forget him.* "Maxy," she groaned as she looped her arms around his powerful neck. Emma molded herself into Massimo's hard body, feeling the outline of how much he wanted her.

MASSIMO COULDN'T BELIEVE Emma was in his arms again. It wasn't a dream that he would wake up from frustrated and in need of a cold shower. How many of those had he taken since he last held her lethal body in Rome? She was here in his private domain. He never brought his women here. He'd never taken a woman to his bed here at the palace. And somehow, it felt right that it was Emma who would share his bed, if only for this one night.

Holding her seductive body in his aching arms, her soft lips parted, inviting him to reacquaint himself with her mouth, her taste. He was bound by an archaic law and the oath he swore to honor when he ascended the throne. But was he not entitled to some happiness?

Her fingers were at the buttons of his vest, then his shirt, tugging. He brushed her hands away and unfastened the remainder of his shirt. "Not here, Red. Come with me," he breathed against her petal-soft, coral lips.

"Okay," she whispered.

Raising his mouth from hers, he gazed into her smoldering green eyes. Massimo slipped her hand in his and guided her through his apartment. She stopped and pulled him to her parted lips. He dragged her petite body into him and hurried toward his bedroom suite. He thrust his tongue into her sweet inviting mouth while he half carried her through the circular foyer. A crystal chandelier above cast a soft yellow glow. The white and gilt double doors to his bedroom were open.

Emma pulled away. Her lips, wet from his kisses she said, "Wow—just wow." Her green eyes widened. "You have a crown over your bed."

His groin heated, and he needed to kiss her lustrous lips again. Massimo tipped his head and shrugged his shoulder. "I know, but it's home," he teased. He slipped the leather strap of her purse over her head, dropping the bag on one of the watered silk wing chairs by the fireplace.

Emma pulled his shirt out of his waistband but he brushed her hands away and spun her around, dragging her zipper down while kissing the creamy satin-smooth skin of her graceful back. She turned and shimmied her shoulders. The dress slipped down the curves of her petite body. She wore a beige scrap of lace thong, and he couldn't help but grab her firm buttocks, pulling her against his throbbing erection. Emma reached behind her to unclasp her bra.

"No, wait, I want to see you spill out of your bra."

Her sexy laugh floated around them. "Yes, just like the first time in Rome."

"Yes, exactly." He slid the silky beige straps of her matching bra down her arms. The clasp parted, freeing her ample breasts. The frilly lace fell to the floor as he cupped her swollen flesh. Her jasmine scent floated around him as he stroked his thumbs over her pink nipples. "These need my undivided attention." He bent his head to kiss the silken swell, sucking first one erect nipple into his hungry mouth, enjoying the feeling as her excited flesh tightened before moving to the other. Her fingers moved through his hair, clenching and unclenching, bringing him closer. He smiled before he nipped the crest of the breast in his mouth.

Her groan set his blood on fire, and his erection pressed uncomfortably against his zipper. Emma unbuttoned his waistband, and Massimo moved her hands away. He lifted Emma in his arms and carried her to his bed.

"Will you be able to find me between all of this bedding?" She pulled him to her, looping her arms around his neck.

"Red, I will find you… anywhere."

Her lips parted, inviting him to kiss her. Massimo sucked the center of her full lower lip, running his tongue over it. Her fingers played at the nape of his neck. He kissed her once more before laying her in the center of his bed. He would go slow and drag this out. Massimo calmed himself by removing his cufflinks and placed them on the night table. Then he unzipped his pants, slipped off his shirt, and dropped his pants and boxers. He drank in her beauty—the indent of her waist, her soft belly, and the curve of her hips as she lay on his blue duvet.

She pushed herself up on her elbows, and her breasts rose and fell in her excitement. He knelt on the bed and threaded his fingers through the thick red mass of her hair.

"You're more naked than me now." She pouted.

"Don't worry, Red. I'll get that thong off you soon enough, but right now, I need to feast on your body."

Her smile almost undid him, wondering if slow was really possible. In Rome, it never had been. The one time they'd ventured into the city—because she'd wanted to toss a coin into the Trevi Fountain for good luck and to ensure a return to Rome—Emma was unaware that his guards and Nicolo followed at a discreet distance. She'd laughed and, with her right hand, tossed a bunch of coins over her left shoulder. "What about you? You have to throw a coin in for good luck and a return to Rome." He hadn't understood.

"Here, I have three more coins," she'd said, taking them from her purse and giving them to him. He'd faced away and tossed them over his left shoulder into the fountain, content to act like a tourist—happy too that she didn't know who he really was. She'd thrown her arms around his neck, pressing her soft body into his as she'd whispered in his ear, "Let's go behind the statue...and." Her tongue traced his ear. He'd grabbed her hand, and they'd hurried back to the hotel and the presidential suite instead.

Now, here at the palace in his bedroom, he cupped her breasts. "The perfect handful," he said and watched as her eyes darkened with pleasure. Her nipples grew, and he had to trace the texture of one with his tongue. Emma combed her fingers through his hair, holding his head to her and pressed her breasts to him. He kissed her silky flesh, sucking and licking the nipple into a diamond hard point, before he kissed the valley between her breasts on his way to her other nipple.

She writhed under him. "Massimo, please..." She ran her hands over his back, digging her fingers into his buttocks.

He nudged her legs apart as his hand slowly drifted down her sensuous body.

"Yes, I can't wait. Feel me."

Massimo fought his own passion. He couldn't wait much longer as his hand slipped over her silky-smooth belly and lower. His fingers brushed the top of her lacy, sexy thong. He touched the patch of springy red curls. Emma lifted her hips in a silent plea. He slid his finger into her. Wet heat enveloped him.

She tugged him from her breasts. "Kiss me."

He did, taking her mouth at first with a gentle sweep of his lips. She opened to him, and he gladly thrust his tongue to entwine with hers. Their teeth clashed. Her silken arms wrapped around him, pulling him closer. The taste of her sweet mouth was better than he could remember without going mad. Her body was curvier than before, or was it that she had always been perfection? She held him to her, her coral-colored nail-polished fingers clutching and pulling him to her.

He needed her heat surrounding him. Massimo was quick grabbing the foil packet from the night table. Ripping it open, he rolled the condom on his throbbing erection. With one sure thrust, he buried himself into her welcoming body.

"Oh, Maxy, you feel so good."

"It's going to get a lot better when I'm fully in you," he rasped, then grabbed her ankle and dragged her leg to his shoulder.

With each thrust, Emma moaned louder sliding her other leg up and resting her knee on his shoulder. "Oh yes, yes." She screamed and her eyes flew open.

He lost himself in the green flame of her gaze. Buried deep in his redheaded beauty, he groaned as a warm tingling began in his lower back, radiating around his hips and into his groin. Emma's pulsing waves of pleasure engulfed him in ecstasy. Massimo kissed her, savoring the feel of her legs once more wrapped around his waist. Then he rose from the bed and went to dispose of the condom.

Coming back into the room, moonlight silvered her seductive body, and his groin hardened once again. He strolled to the bed and pulled her into his arms. *She's here in my bed... She has to go home.* He kissed her brow. "Red, you know this is not good for either of us. I have to do what I must, and it is a life without you."

"I know, Maxy. Let's not talk about that. All I want are the memories of this one night to keep forever. In the morning, I'll go home."

Massimo lay on his side, resting his head in the palm of his hand. He watched Emma as she slept. Everything good in his world lay next to him. Her beauty and her sense of humor were great, but her sexy way definitely kept him wanting more. He had to let her go. He couldn't hurt her anymore. Her words haunted him. "Give me this one night to keep forever." This time together wasn't good for either of them. It reminded him of the hell he'd lived through this past year. How many times had he forced himself not to find her? Craving only her and not free to commit.

Tonight was all they had, and he would make the best of it. He slid his hand down the sultry curves of her body, stopping to feel the weight of a breast, before moving down, his fingers spread over the smooth flesh of her torso to her belly.

Emma moaned and separated her thighs in invitation to his hand. "Mmm, yes."

He covered the red patch of hair between her legs before his finger found her sensitive bundle of nerves.

"Oh, Massimo. You're real. It's not a dream."

"Yes, Emma, I'm here. I'm real. Touch me and feel my desire for you. Soon, I will make you feel everything I have for you." Massimo kissed her belly, sliding his lips lower and lower. More than anything, he needed to taste her desire for him. To memorize her beauty in his brain and her taste on his tongue.

HIS VIRILE MASCULINE scent drifted around Emma, and she couldn't hold back the low moans that his lovemaking brought out in her. She loved everything Massimo did. Her body burned with intense need, spreading from her belly to where his long finger thrust deep into her. Finding her g-spot, he stroked the sensitive nerve endings.

Emma sighed in anticipation as his broad shoulders wedged between her spread thighs. He kissed first one leg, then the other. In Rome, he had been the first to show her this kind of pleasure. Now, she lifted her hips to him, and heat engulfed her as his lips traveled to her very center. His tongue traced erotic patterns over her wet, heated flesh. She writhed in his powerful arms as she fought to hold back the waves of pleasure, wanting the incredible sensations to go on and never stop.

She couldn't control herself. She was wild, thrashing her head from side to side on the satin pillow. "Yes, yes. Oh, Massimo, now I know you're real," she cried out, giving into the erotic waves of rapture.

"Grrr." Massimo kept her spread wide. His dark head was at her center, and his broad, muscular shoulders wedged between her thighs.

Her heart raced, and she couldn't wait for what he would do next.

He stopped.

She sobbed, "No." Her fingers clutched at his thick, black hair. "I'm so close. Don't stop! Please, make me come," she panted in quick breaths of air.

In the muted light from the chandeliers and the night table lamps, he lifted his head, and his sapphire-blue eyes burned into her. A slow smile spread across his lips. "I want to feel and taste you come," he said before he slipped his powerful hands under her, lifting her higher to his mouth. Massimo began again.

"Yes, just like that," Emma implored before she raised her arms over her head, arching her back. She was wild as his tongue traced her folds, then Massimo sucked her clit into his mouth. "Oh, dear God, yesss," she screamed as she came on his tongue. Long, sweet waves of pulsing pleasure rolled through her. Emma's legs relaxed. Her body felt weightless. There was only Massimo. He traced her excited flesh once more, keeping her open to him. Her abdomen tightened, and her fingers slipped through his hair. She couldn't help cupping his head, holding him to her. Panting, moaning,

"Maxy, yes, do that again," she screamed when a second orgasm, more intense than the first, snuck up on her.

Massimo stayed where she needed him most until the last shudder of pleasure left her body. Her legs slipped from his broad shoulders. Her breathing slowly returned to normal, and he kissed her belly once more before he sat up, taking her along with him. Leaning his broad back against the blue-velvet headboard, he reached for the condom he'd placed on the night table earlier. His hair tousled from her fingers and the scent of her on him, he said, "Are you ready for more, Red?"

She eagerly nodded. "Yes, I want you in me." *Don't tell him that you're on the pill. Keep it to yourself.*

CHAPTER 4

$\mathcal{M}$assimo loved her excitement as he ripped the packet open. Emma scooted onto his thighs while he rolled the latex onto his throbbing erection. She smiled at him. "Mmm, I like this position."

"I knew you would," he said, lifting her over his length. She straddled him, her hands onto his biceps. She slowly slid down his engorged flesh, taking all of him into her. Her eyes closed, and a smile spread across her kiss-swollen lips. Emma was beautiful the way she tipped her head back, exposing her graceful neck. Long, red hair brushed his thighs. He caught his fingers in the silky strands, and savored the feeling of how snug and deep in her tight passage he was.

"Ahh, Massimo," she moaned and opened her emerald eyes.

His gaze held her captive just as she held him in her body. "You know, Red, I love your breasts," he said. Lowering his head, his teeth grazed one nipple before he gave it a lazy lick.

"Mmmm, yes," Emma purred as she pressed her breast into his mouth. She cupped his head, and Massimo couldn't help nipping her.

"Oh yes, Maxy." She shifted her hips before rising on her knees to slowly lower herself down, taking all of him into her again.

He grabbed her toned butt cheeks in his hands to lift and lower her on his shaft.

"Oh, yes." She pulsed around him. Her inner muscles tightened, holding him in her.

His face contorted at the pleasure of her tightness. He lifted and lowered her several more times before the tingling in his back spread around his abdomen. He throbbed deep in her body.

"Maxy, I love how you fill me."

Her words were his undoing, and he pulsed before he erupted, shooting his hot seed into her.

"Maxy…" She panted and fell forward on him, spreading kisses along his chest, reaching to kiss his lips as their breaths mingled. He held her in his arms, his fingers tangled in her lustrous, red hair. Emma stroked his chest, her fingers making patterns in his hair. Her small, pink tongue circled a flat, dark nipple before she rolled to his side. She rested her head on his shoulder. He felt her lips on his neck, kissing him.

He brushed her hair from her face, stroking her lower lip with his thumb as he kissed her damp temple. "I'll be right back." He left the bed to dispose of the condom. When he returned, he found her curled on her side, asleep. He draped his arm around her tiny waist and tucked his knees under her. Closing his eyes, he breathed in her jasmine scent.

~

EMMA STIRRED, opening her eyes. She instantly remembered where she was, rolled over, and stroked the silky black hair on Massimo's chest. He tugged her to him. "You woke up. Are you hungry?"

She loved to tease him. "For more of this? Yes."

"Always, Red, but what about food?"

"Oh. I could go for something to eat," she said, sliding her hand over the rock-hard muscles of his abdomen.

Gold flecks sparked in Massimo's gaze, igniting a flame in the blue depths of his eyes. "I'll order shrimp and lobster, then we can continue with your idea in the shower."

"Food and shower sex. What more could a girl want?"

He led her into an enormous oval-shaped ensuite. Glass and mirrors covered the walls. The floor was white marble and in the middle of the room, a crystal chandelier hung over a round, freestanding tub with spa jets. Off to one side were a marble and glass-enclosed shower. He turned one of the several knobs and from overhead, rainwater flowed. A marble bench had been carved into the center of one wall. Emma slipped her hand into his and led him to the bench that resembled an open seashell. All the while, a warm, gentle mist touched their skin from the overhead shower.

She nudged him to sit, then knelt before him. He looked like a Roman statue, his sculpted muscles bulging. Massimo's olive skin glistened from the rain shower. Beads of water clung to his broad chest, running through the smattering of dark hair, glistening like diamonds. The water ran over his flat nipples, and one rivulet led down the center of his torso over the hard muscles of his abdomen. She watched, and her throat dried. Her pelvis burned and flooded with her own desire.

Emma laid her hands on his thighs to spread his muscled legs, marveling at how they reminded her of tree trunks. She inched closer between his knees, and his glorious erection grew. Emma gazed up at him, smiling. He held her eyes as one dark brow rose. She nodded, taking him in her hand.

Her thumb skimmed the velvet softness of his engorged head.

Massimo leaned against the marble wall of the shower. It excited her to look at him as she used her mouth to bring him pleasure. At one point, he reached for her head, his long fingers tangling in her hair in a similar way that she had when he brought her to orgasm. His shout filled the air, making her giddy to give him the same kind of pleasure he brought her.

He grabbed a bar of soap with his monogram on it and lathered his hands. They washed each other with the distinct fragrance of sandalwood from the soap. He lifted her to wrap her legs around him and they made love against the marble wall, the warm spray of water soothing them.

Afterward, Massimo gave her one of his shirts to wear. Earlier her clothes had been taken to be cleaned and pressed. He wore a pair of faded jeans. He kissed the palm of her hand before entwining his fingers with hers. She leaned against his side. Barefoot, they walked to the sitting room. While they'd showered, their food had been set out for them.

The couch was overstuffed and looked very comfortable. A sideboard held ornate sterling-silver warming trays. Massimo handed her a china plate with gold-fluted edges before he took one for himself.

Emma lifted the lid on a warming tray. "Yummy, the smell is fabulous. Grilled shrimp on a bed of rice pilaf." She spooned some onto her plate.

Massimo poured her a glass of champagne. "It's one in the morning, and I'm famished for food, that is."

She giggled. "Me too. I haven't eaten since breakfast this morning, technically yesterday... before I found out you were coming to the ministry."

His eyes narrowed. "Were you nervous to see me?"

"Yes."

They sat on the couch, their knees touching, and ate. Emma bit into a tender shrimp, then took a bite-sized wedge of cheese from his plate and popped it into her mouth.

"Do you like your work?"

"Yes, I enjoy it very much. I get to travel to different countries. When we met in Rome, I had just attended a seminar from the World Heritage Foundation on Roman cement. What about you?" she asked, gazing into his blue eyes.

"I was scheduled to address the general assembly at the United Nations when my plane was grounded after ash from the volcano eruption made it dangerous to fly."

"Very impressive." She took a sip of her champagne.

"I find what you do fascinating." Massimo pushed a stray red curl behind her ear. "In Rome, we didn't talk much about our lives, like two ships passing in the night. It pleased me immensely that a beautiful, independent woman treated me like a regular person and not a king. You didn't know who I was, and I could be myself. I liked that. I'm curious. You said you hadn't been in a serious relationship for two years?"

"Well, there wasn't actually a *relationship*. Josh was my next-door neighbor. He's a year older than me, and we grew up together. I had a crush on him. He was my first date, and he escorted me to my high school prom. Then he left to go to college in Arizona, while I stayed in New York."

Emma smoothed her hair back from her face. "We didn't see each other for a long time. Somehow, we both ended up at MIT in grad school. We spent all our time together as a couple while we were in Massachusetts. I fell in love with him."

She pursed her lips. "He thought it was—Emma made air quotes—"casual…Then he married someone else. Someone who–" Emma shrugged. "I guess money and power were more important to him. Her family name and her father's company seemed to be the key to Josh's heart." She snickered. "Her name is… also Emma, but with a much more prestigious last name." She bit the corner of her lip. "As I'd said, we were neighbors. My father and his father were friends and work buddies in the fire department. I had to go to their wedding and suffer through it. It killed me to be at that wedding, watching them exchange vows and pretend that it wasn't destroying me."

He brought her hand up to his lips. "You are a very brave woman to do that. Keeping your feelings buried is a very royal thing to do."

"Well, it stinks," she snapped before taking her plate of food from her lap and placing it on the coffee table. "I know you need to marry someone with a royal bloodline and provide an heir. The buzz around the ministry is that you've chosen someone, and the engagement is imminent." She tucked her feet under her.

"This is what you want to talk about?" Massimo grumbled.

"I've told you something very personal. It's only fair that you tell me something too."

He sighed and turned away, no longer meeting her eyes. "Yes… there is someone I've chosen. It's pretty much settled. We will marry in August. I just have to make it official by putting a ring on Luisa's finger."

"Luisa?" she echoed. She couldn't take a breath.

His brow furrowed. "What is wrong? You are ghost white. What has happened?"

What a joke this is. "That's very interesting. Fate, destiny, whatever you wish to call it making me the brunt of their joke. Did you know that my middle name is Louise?"

"No, I did not. I am truly sorry. Emma, I hope you realize that I am living in my own special hell. Duty, honor, and traditions…I wish it could have been different for you and me."

"Massimo, I never expected the explosion of feelings we've shared. For me, I say that alone is better, without the pain of longing for you." *Both men left me for another woman.*

Massimo brushed his lips over her temple. "Who is in your life, Emma?"

"I don't want your pity, Massimo. I have my father… my family." *And I have my son.*

"Never pity, Emma. Admiration comes to mind. You are a competent, independent woman."

"No more serious convos."

"An abbreviation for conversation?" Massimo reached for the remote on the coffee table. "Then no more convo." He aimed the remote at the cabinet, and a flat-screen TV rose out of it.

"Remember when you taught me about games?" He wiggled his brows at her. "Wanna play?"

"Yes… I think so. What do you have in mind?"

"Do you recollect when you accused me of having too many holes in my general knowledge of all things stupid?"

She giggled at the look on his face and nodded. "Yes."

The first question came up on the screen. She shifted her gaze to look at him, lifting one brow. "This is not regular trivia."

"No, it isn't. We are going to play naughty trivia. Be warned, Ms. Harris. This time, there won't be any lack of knowledge."

Emma nodded again as a smile spread over her lips. "Name something on your body you wish were smaller?" She leaned into him before she said, "I know something on your body that's just the right size."

"Do you? Come… show me, Red."

Emma rested her hand on his bare chest, breathing in the

sandalwood scent and rubbing her fingers through the smattering of silky black hair. She traced the thin line of hair over his abdomen, lower until his jeans got in the way. She bit the corner of her bottom lip as she unfastened his waistband. Slowly, she slid the zipper down.

Massimo lifted her to straddle his lap. This was one of their favorite positions. *How could we have a favorite anything? He's marrying someone else, and I go home in the morning.* He slipped his hands under the silk shirt he'd given her to wear. Her nipples tightened, and she couldn't get enough. He pulled her snug against him, kissing her neck as she held onto his broad shoulders. This time that they shared would be the last for the rest of their lives. Her eyes stung. *Don't you dare cry, just live for now.*

He grazed a nipple with his teeth, and she tangled her fingers in his hair, holding him to her. "Oh, yes, I like that," she moaned, riding him faster and faster.

Her subconscious needled her, and all Emma wanted was for Massimo to regret his decision. She had to harden her heart. Move on. He would do what duty dictated, and she would have to live with that and the knowledge that men always left her. She would never tell Massimo about Steven.

The sun rose, lighting the bedroom with pink and salmon streaks of light. Massimo cradled her in his strong arms one last time. Just before she rose from the bed, she reached for her cell phone. She looked at the screen, then shut it.

"I don't recall you being so dedicated to your phone when we were in Rome."

"Oh well, I'm not… just…checking the time," she said, averting her eyes.

Emma dressed in the same green outfit she'd arrived in, freshly cleaned and pressed. Massimo waited for her in the sitting room. Tall and lean, the suit he wore couldn't hide his powerful body. "I would prefer you not remove yourself from the hospital project."

"I have to go home. You have qualified people here, and they can step in." *He can't find out about Steven. Now more than ever. I can't lose my son to him. I know I made the right decision not to tell him.*

"I hate it. Stay. Take the position of liaison. Then, once the project is over, you can go home. I don't want to say goodbye yet."

"No." Emma cupped his cheek. "You know that it would be difficult for me to stay in Malagra. I can't. You must understand. I have to go home now." *I won't be the other woman.* She shook her head. "Massimo, I don't... trust myself... to stay out of your bed. Once you're married, it would be impossible for me to be here." She snapped, "I find it unfair of you to ask."

His gaze burned into her. "Yes, I know you would. If this were another time, I would find a way to keep you here. Perhaps the dungeon," he drawled.

"Dungeon?" She gasped, shaking her head. She took a step back from him as fear curled in her belly and ran up her spine. She was tempted to run. *He doesn't know about Steven, be calm.*

"Emma Harris, you are still and always will be the woman of my heart."

"Don't say that," she warned.

He dragged her into his arms and kissed her for the last time. "Please just go. A car is waiting to take you back to your hotel."

CHAPTER 5

Emma and her team from Collins and Collins sat in the business-class cabin of the commercial jet. She buckled her seatbelt.

As the jet sped down the runway, her co-worker sighed. "It's good to be going home."

"I can't wait. I emailed all our reports to the office, and I'm going to take an extended weekend. Four days, just me and Steven."

"Oh, you must miss him so much. My husband and I have similar plans. Some rest and relaxation are definitely needed. All we did for two weeks was work in the city. I would have liked to do some sightseeing."

The jet reached cruising altitude, and the captain turned off the fasten seat belt sign. Emma gazed out the window, and her thoughts turned to the King of Malagra. It was futile to wish that Massimo would find a way for them to be together other than his desire to have her as the other woman. She was confident she'd made the right choice, keeping Steven from him. Massimo would never find out about their child. It was best that way. *I have to move forward, alone with only my son. Will the ache in my heart for Massimo ever lessen?*

She would find a way to heal her broken heart. When she'd learned she was pregnant, it was her decision to keep her baby. In Rome, Massimo had said all he could give her was that time they'd shared. Emma understood now. He clearly could never give her more than a few stolen hours. She would move on without him. She had to.

Emma wouldn't be the other woman, nor would she lose her son to Massimo. The article she'd read about his great-great-great-grandfather taking his son, the crown prince's baby, from its mother turned her blood to ice. She'd clicked out of that story without reading further, but the fear lingered. Was it a threat when he said he would like to keep her in the dungeon?

Emma closed her eyes, listening to the low hum of the jet. She didn't regret one moment of the night she'd spent in Massimo's arms. She would tuck that away with all her other memories of their time together. She mentally squared her shoulders, prepared to move on. She knew in the depths of her soul without a doubt she could never be near him without falling into his bed. Soon he would belong to Luisa. She had to make a life for herself and her baby boy. *He's marrying someone else...Maybe if I keep saying it— I can believe it. I will not think of him. I will not think of him. No, no, no.*

Once the plane landed, Emma retrieved her car from the long-term parking garage at the airport and drove to the three-story brownstone she was born in and shared with her father in Brooklyn. Her mother had died when she was in elementary school, so it was only the two of them. When she found out she was pregnant, she had told her dad that the baby's father would not and could not be in the picture. He'd suggested that they remodel the first floor— bump out the back of the house and add a mini suite for her and the baby. It included a bedroom with a separate sitting room and an ensuite for her. An adjoining nursery and a bedroom with a small sitting area and a private bath for a nanny. The remainder of the first floor stayed the same, with the living room, dining room, and gourmet kitchen.

Emma hurried up the front brick steps to the double wood and glass doors of the main entrance. Walking into the vestibule, she opened the entry door. "I'm home," she said, leaving her suitcase, coat, and purse in the foyer. She hurried into the cozy living room.

Her dad lowered the TV volume before rising from the brown leather couch. "Welcome home, sweetheart," he said, his arms extended to give her a hug.

"Hi, Dad." She kissed him on his smoothly shaven cheek. "I'm so happy to be home. How is Steven?" she asked over her shoulder already heading down the hallway toward the nursery and her bedroom.

"He may have grown a few inches while you were away." Her dad chuckled behind her.

"I'm never leaving him again."

Emma walked into the bright and airy white and sky-blue nursery. The nanny was folding some of Steven's clothes at his changing table. She went to the crib. Steven, dressed in a yellow knit romper, lay on his back, playing with his toes. "Hello, my precious little boy. Mama's home."

Steven gave her a drooly grin. Emma picked him up, breathing in his baby powder fresh scent and kissed him.

"Hello, Miss Harris. Welcome home," the nanny said as she continued putting the baby's clothes away.

"Thank you. I missed him so much," Emma said, cuddling Steven in her arms. "I've arranged to take the next four days off from work. I have a video conference later today, then I'm free."

"Oh, perfect. If it's okay with you, then I'll visit my sister in New Jersey."

"Yes, of course. I plan on staying home and doing nothing more than relaxing. I'll take Steven for long walks to the park so we can enjoy this unusually mild weather."

MASSIMO STOOD on the stone floor of the terrace by his bedroom. The palace was built on the edge of a cliff, and his residence had a vast view of the Mediterranean Sea. He clasped his hands behind his back. It was late afternoon, and he stared out at the glistening aqua water. Emma had flown home the day before. *She made her choice, and now I have to do what I must do. I cannot put this off any longer.* He strolled back into his bedroom and over to the nightstand. He glanced down at the antique red velvet ring box before picking it up. Earlier in the day, he'd asked Nicolo to retrieve the ring from the palace vaults.

He flipped the lid and let out a long breath as he looked at the square-cut emerald ring surrounded by clear, round diamonds. The ring had belonged to his grandmother and soon enough, it would grace Luisa's hand. At dinner last week, he had asked Luisa what type of ring she would like, something new or something from a previous queen. Luisa had expressed an interest in the ring his grandmother wore when she was engaged to his grandfather.

Massimo had to stop delaying the inevitable. What was he, a child dragging his feet so as not to do something unpleasant? He'd invited Luisa to the palace. Tonight, he would formally propose to her, placing the ring on her finger. He snapped the lid shut and set the red velvet box back on his nightstand.

He knew Luisa was just waiting for this formality to be

over. At that same dinner last week, she'd mentioned she had chosen the perfect outfit to wear when their engagement was announced to the people of Malagra and the world. Once he slid the ring on her finger, they could plan for an August wedding with all the pomp and circumstances due to the king and his new queen. That would give everyone five months to make arrangements and get their calendars in order. *Give me the opportunity to adjust to the bitter taste of duty and a loveless marriage. I know this is right for Malagra. I need an heir.*

Massimo left his apartment. He walked down the hall, bypassed the elevator, and veered toward the main staircase down to the second floor. One wing of the palace held his office and executive staff for the king. Two footmen opened the double doors that led to his private office. The drapes were drawn wide to let in the late-afternoon light. A round blue-and-gold Persian rug covered the center of the room where his highly polished walnut desk stood. Bookcases lined one wall. He sat in his leather high-back chair. His computer monitor was set up on his desk, and he waited to join the video conference. The lead architect on the hospital project, as well as Gino and Mr. James Collins, would be present.

Nicolo walked in. "Sir, the video call is connected, and everyone is waiting for you."

"Good. Put it through."

His monitor lit up. "Hello."

"Your Majesty," Jim Collins said, "I am delighted to personally update you on the progress of the hospital. I received the reports from Ms. Harris and her team yesterday. Ms. Harris did a thorough job, and we are going to implement her latest recommendations. I understand that you were able to view the overall model and the individual major areas."

"Yes, I'm pleased with the design. I thought Ms. Harris would have stayed on to see the project to the end, rather than turn it over to someone else. Although she assured me that the new person is qualified."

"Your Majesty, I was thrilled that Ms. Harris was able to do the preliminary work—she made sure the site was perfect and then had the architect make necessary changes based on her specifications."

"I'm aware of that," Massimo said in a level voice, never giving anything away. He couldn't simply command her presence when it wasn't good for either of them.

"It is quite impossible to ask her to stay in Malagra. I'm grateful that she agreed to do this major part of the project at all since she just returned from maternity leave."

What? Massimo leaned forward in his chair. The muscles in his arms tensed. "Did you say maternity leave?" Years of hiding his emotions and guarding his feelings from public view, paid off now.

"Yes, Your Majesty; she has a son. I wasn't sure she would leave the baby."

Massimo couldn't believe what Mr. Collins said. *Why didn't she tell me?* "Under the circumstances, that is quite understandable… How old is the baby?"

"I think he's four months old. You understand why we won't ask her to return to Malagra? She will have to oversee the project from New York, as agreed."

"Yes. Thank you for your time. You can schedule our next conference with my chief aide, Nicolo." Massimo ended the video feed. Gino remained on the video call once the others disconnected. "You knew?" Massimo asked his cousin.

"Yes, she spoke with the nanny a few times a day."

"I see. Are you happy with the person she chose to lead the project?"

"Yes, sir. I am. Ms. Harris selected him herself and went

over and over his qualifications. She assured me that he was the best person to replace her."

"Very well, Gino." Massimo clicked off the call and walked into his aide's office.

"Nicolo, get my pilot. I'm going to New York today. Now."

"Yes, sir," Nicolo said, already reaching for his phone.

"Find out where Emma Harris lives. Get the address to me immediately. She has a son. I want details."

"Yes, sir."

Massimo left his office and went back to his apartment. He couldn't understand what had just happened. *Oh, yes, you understand. First, she didn't want me to know she was here. Now, she keeps her baby from me.* Was he a father or was Emma pregnant when they'd hooked up? If he were a father, why hadn't she said anything? He wasn't very patient. He needed answers at once.

His fury built the more he thought about their recent night together. This was the second time in as many days that her deceit got under his skin. *Oh, that sweet, innocent face and that lethal body. Oh, what a deceitful redheaded witch she is.*

He strolled into his dressing room and found his head valet preparing his clothes for dinner with Luisa. "Delay that. I'm traveling to New York within the hour."

His valet bowed his head. "Yes, sir. I'll pack your bags."

"I won't need more than you attending me. This is not an official trip."

"Very well, sir." He bowed once more, then went to prepare for the flight.

Massimo paced around his bedroom, something he never did. The King of Malagra didn't pace. He called Luisa and cancelled their dinner.

Fifteen minutes later, Nicolo walked into Massimo's

private apartment. "Your Majesty, I have the address and the name of her child. Steven Max Harris."

Massimo grunted. *Maxy.* "Good work. Are we ready?"

"Yes, sir. Your car is waiting in the courtyard. Everything is prepared. The flight crew is already on board your plane, as well as the royal guard."

"Good," he said, walking out of his apartment.

Nine hours later, Nicolo climbed the brick steps of Emma's brownstone ahead of Massimo and rang the doorbell. He stood flanked by two of his bodyguards, waiting for entry. He saw Emma through the leaded glass door. Dressed in leggings and a long sleeve shirt—her lustrous red hair was tied in a high ponytail. She looked like a teenager and not the competent engineer she was, or more so, the deceitful woman he couldn't forget. The mother of his child.

CHAPTER 6

Two black SUVs were stopped on the street outside of her home. Emma hesitated, her eyes rounding when she saw Massimo. Tall, dark, handsome, and in a blue sport jacket. He wore a collarless shirt and cream-colored pants. *Oh no, why is he here?*

Nicolo and the men standing behind Massimo wore dark suits, and each had a button on their lapel. Her fingers trembled as she reached for the knob of the interior door. Taking a fortifying breath, Emma swung the entry door wide. "What are you doing here?" she said, not a bit surprised at the quiver in her voice.

Massimo stepped into the vestibule. His tall, broad-shouldered frame took up much of the space. One dark brow rose, and his anger-filled blue eyes pierced her. "Surely you know why I flew halfway around the world." He leaned down to her, his nostrils flared. "I came for my son."

Her heart raced. "No. Who told you?"

Massimo strode past her and stood in the foyer. "Where is he?" he demanded.

His menacing voice sent fear racing through her body.

Emma didn't care. She stepped in front of him, stretching her neck to look into his sapphire-blue eyes, preventing Massimo from going down the hall. "No. You can't have him. He's my son."

Massimo nodded to the two men flanking him that were almost as tall and broad shouldered as he was. One man moved to stand in front of her, blocking her path, while Massimo—the king—stepped around her.

Her worst nightmare was playing out right now in her home. "No, no please. Don't do this. He's sleeping," Emma pleaded, wringing her hands.

Massimo's head snapped in her direction, eyes narrow, before he turned and peered down the hallway. Emma never saw him look so fierce as he stalked through her home to the nursery. She took a step to follow, and the guard put his arm out.

"Get out of my way," she gritted between clenched teeth.

Massimo never turned. He continued walking toward the back of the house. Over his shoulder, he commanded, "Let her pass."

The guard moved, and Emma hurried after Massimo. He walked up to the crib. Emma's body shook as she watched him. She clutched her chest as he stood there, looking down at Steven. Her son had black hair, the exact inky color as his father's. Massimo bent over the crib and lifted her sleeping son up to cradle him in his powerful arms.

Emma cried out, "Massimo, please don't take him from me."

He turned to his bodyguards. "Leave us," he said in a low voice, and his men immediately walked out of the nursery.

Massimo held his son. Gradually, a smile lifted the corners of his full lips, brightening his face for the first time since entering her home as he gazed down at Steven. Emma took a calming breath. She couldn't miss the love on Massimo's handsome face as he gazed at the sleeping baby in his arms. He brushed the knuckle of his pointing finger over Steven's cheek, then over his tiny, fisted hand. The baby slept on as Massimo gently held him.

In a hushed tone, he asked, "Why did you keep him from me?" Still looking at the baby, Massimo slowly shook his head before he lifted his gaze to her. "You were never going to tell me?"

Emma saw the anger directed at her in the depths of his stormy blue eyes. "No," was all she said. *He's going to marry someone else. He sent me away and will marry Lady Luisa. I owe him nothing.*

His eyes flared. "We made love. I held you in my arms and all that time, you were keeping my son from me." His voice rumbled.

"Don't wake him," she whispered, ignoring his accusations.

"That's all you have to say? You're coming back to Malagra with me."

She kept her voice low, even with the icy fingers of fear racing up her spine. "I can't. My life is here. You were very clear when you told me that you are bound by the oath you took. You must honor your duty and the laws of your country. I need to do what's right for me and my son."

"He's my son, and you have no right to keep me from him. I want to bond with him."

She frowned, her eyes narrowing. "Steven is my son. I was the one who chose to keep him. You gave up your rights in Rome when you neglected to tell me who you really are."

"I never lied to you. I was honest with you.… unlike you," he sneered. "When I closed the door to that suite, I left my heart with you…and now it seems my son as well."

They faced each other in the center of the nursery, the

chasm between them insurmountable while Massimo held Steven. "Come back with me," he commanded.

"How will that work? You're marrying someone else. You'll have children with her. Steven and I will not be kept hidden in the shadows of your life."

"I'm not asking you to do that. I'm telling you—I will get to know my son."

The baby whimpered and opened his eyes. Massimo looked down at Steven. "His eyes are blue... the exact shade as mine."

"Massimo, let him sleep. We can talk in the other room."

"There will be no discussion, Emma. I'm taking him back to Malagra where he belongs. I want you to come too."

Her heart beat so fast, she felt dizzy. "Give him to me," Emma demanded, taking her son from his arms. She cradled Steven to her, swaying to help him fall back to sleep. Once he was sleeping, Emma looked at Massimo and said, "You can't have him."

"That's where you're wrong. He is my son, and he belongs to Malagra. You can come if you wish, but he leaves with me."

"When you left me in Rome, you just went on about your business. I chose to keep him." She shook her head and fought not to cry. "I didn't know who you were or how to find you. The medallion you gave me..." She shrugged. "I searched the internet to no avail. I couldn't find anything about—"

"Once you found out, you could have told me. But no, not you. Instead, you lay in my arms that night at the palace and, in the morning, you walked away. At some point, you could have found a moment to tell me." His face was a mass of rage, as he shouted, "You were going to deny him his birthright."

"You're angry?" She was incredulous.

"I'm trying to understand—"

"There's nothing to understand. You're marrying someone else. Then, you have the nerve to accuse me of denying him something that cannot be his. You've made it clear that my blood isn't royal like hers. Go have children with her. They will be your heirs. But don't take what little I have. Again, I say there's no birthright, and you know it." She hadn't realized she was shouting until Steven cried out in his sleep. Emma held him closer to calm him and herself. Her eyes stung with unshed tears. She lowered her voice, almost unable to talk past the tightness in her throat. "You and I have to be rational about this. Please, Massimo, you mustn't do this to me. He's all I have. You have so much—"

MASSIMO HEARD a male voice bellow through the house, calling for Emma.

Her eyes widened. "Oh no. It's my father. He's home from work. You wait here." She hurried out of the nursery and said,, "Dad, it's okay, I'm all right, and so is Steven. See, we're fine. I'll explain everything."

"Who are these men?" he shouted.

Massimo walked out of the nursery. "Nicolo, I am safe here. There is no need for all of you to be in the house."

The man that stared back at him—Emma's father—was in his mid-fifties and as tall as he was with a head of red hair. Emma's dad put an arm around her shoulders and looked down at Steven as his guards left the house.

For a moment, he said nothing. Once Nicolo and the men were gone, her dad looked at him before he said, "The father, I presume."

Massimo strode over to him and extended his hand. "Yes, I acknowledge I am Steven's father."

Emma's dad shook his hand.

"Let's go into the living room," Emma said as she cradled Steven and led the way. Once in there, she turned to her father. "I would like you to meet… His Majesty, King Massimo of Malagra, Steven's father."

Emma's father nodded, his brows coming together before he walked over to the bar in the corner of the living room. He grabbed a cut crystal decanter filled with amber liquid. "Scotch, Your Majesty," he asked.

"Yes." He inclined his head. "You may call me Massimo."

Once her dad poured their drinks and downed his, he said to Emma, "Malagra, isn't that where you were working?"

Emma nodded, and Massimo said, "It's complicated."

Steven Harris chuckled. "I'll bet on that. Please call me Steve. Will you excuse my daughter and me for a moment?"

"Yes."

As Emma and her father walked out of the living room, Massimo thought about the woman who'd given birth to his son. She was the only one who could anger him. He'd been furious when he'd learned that she had kept the baby's existence from him. Her audacity, going to bed with him and then leaving, without one word of a child. To see Emma holding her baby and all the love she had for that little boy took the edge off of his fury, although his anger simmered below the surface. He would give her the opportunity to better explain her actions.

He thought about what Emma had said to him. *You left me in Rome and went about your business.* He'd made it clear from the beginning that he couldn't see her again. But now, the fear he saw in her eyes made him stop and think. He walked around the room, stopping to look at the artwork on one wall. His brows furrowed. There were framed drawings. He looked closer. They were signed. Emma, kindergarten, first grade, second grade, all the way through her most recent design of a hospital, graduate school.

Emma came back into the living room without the baby or her father. She slid the pocket door closed, and he watched her. Her head was bent, and she took in a long breath before she straightened and turned to him. "We need to talk seriously, you and I."

"I agree. We need to be honest with each other. I'll go first," he said.

She sat in an overstuffed accent chair opposite him. "Okay, if you insist, *Your Majesty.*"

He clenched his jaw. Another thing he'd never done until Emma Louise Harris came into his life. But the way she said, *Your Majesty*, sounded like a slur and not the honor due to him. He ignored it. "When I left you in Rome, my heart ached for what could never be. At the time, I thought it best not to tell you who I was—a clean break—but in that year, you were never far from my thoughts. I didn't choose to fall in love with you, but I did. And when I saw you in Malagra, I was angry that you didn't let me know you were the lead engineer on the hospital project. My anger didn't last past your first kiss. I know we can't have a life together as a couple... but now, there's Steven, and I don't want to be excluded from my son's life."

"How can this work?" she snapped. Her chest rose with the deep breath she took before she continued, "You say you love me and then threaten to take Steven from me. I read an article about your great great-great-grandfather and his mistress—"

"That was a different time and a different king. I am not him, a tyrant. Emma, you know me."

She furrowed her brow and bit the corner of her lip. He wanted to drag her into his arms, kiss her lips until—he sighed. "You know Steven has a grandmother, aunts, uncles, and an abundance of cousins."

Emma stood and walked away from him. Standing near

the wall of art, she said, "He's just a baby. All he does is sleep and eat. How can he know these people?"

One of Massimo's dark brows lifted. "You don't believe that. This is an important time in a child's development, and I don't want to miss it. I will not miss out on these early years. Emma, all I want is to get to know him. You can come home whenever you want."

"What you said earlier doesn't sound like that."

"I have never lied to you." He covered his heart with his hand. "On my honor as the King of Malagra, you can come home whenever you wish to."

"I want to be clear on this. You do mean me *and* Steven."

He couldn't help how the corners of his mouth lifted. "You're very shrewd. Yes, of course, both of you."

"I want my own room…I won't sleep with you, and I am the only one who will take care of my son. No nanny."

"As you wish."

CHAPTER 7

*E*mma had flown on a private jet before, but nothing prepared her for His Majesty's jet. Everything on board was arranged for the king's comfort and pleasure. His personal chef traveled with him, as well as his valet. The king's chief aide, Nicolo Rana, and a dozen members of the royal guard, along with a separate security team. The two bedrooms onboard were almost as opulent as his apartment at the palace. One bedroom had a crib and a bassinet ready for Steven. All the comforts of home had been provided. She took advantage of the bedroom, so that she could avoid any serious conversations with Massimo.

A flight attendant knocked on her door. "Ms. Harris, His Majesty would like you to know that we will land in thirty minutes."

"Thank you. I'll be ready."

She changed Steven's diaper, then splashed water on her face and brushed her hair, putting it into a ponytail. When she was around Steven lately, she didn't wear earrings and always put her hair up. Last month, he began tugging on her face, especially her ears, and pulling her hair. He'd gripped her hair in his little fist so tight, she feared she'd lose consciousness. When she told her aunt about that, she said, "Oh yes, the grabbing stage."

Massimo waited in the lounge at the front of the plane for her. He'd changed into a three-piece, light-gray suit, his muscular build barely contained in the expensive fabric. His tall height exuded power, making his chiseled features even more desirable. He took Steven and led her to the exit.

"This isn't Santino," Emma said, as they left the luxury of the royal jet.

"No, we are going to my retreat on Isola del Sole, Island of the Sun. It is off the southern coast of Malagra. The castle is one of my favorites. It is where I come to escape and unwind. We will have privacy from the press here. I don't need all the security that I have following me in Santino or if we choose to stay abroad."

In the early morning hours, a warm breeze replaced the tang of jet fuel with the briny fragrance of the Mediterranean Sea. Massimo held Steven and descended the stairs while Emma walked alongside him.

"Okay, if you say so. Just remember we agreed it's only for two weeks… and I'm not sleeping with you." *Definitely no sex. Keep reminding yourself of that.* "You said I can have my own room just for me and Steven. No nanny either."

"Yes, our agreement will be honored. I gave you my word. I want to help care for our son so I can bond with him. I have missed four months, and I don't want to miss any more time with him. No nanny, per se, but you will need some help with the everyday things."

Emma didn't miss the opportunity to needle him. "We don't want your fiancée to get her panties in a twist or be upset with you. Besides, how is she going to react to Steven?" She shifted her eyes to gaze at the clean-shaven olive skin of his profile.

She recognized the anger in his voice. "Luisa is not my fiancée, yet, and everyone will react to Steven as I tell them to. He is my son, after all." Massimo dipped his handsome face closer to her. A hint of his cologne drifted around her as he added, "Red, don't you know…this is an absolute monarchy? My word is law throughout Malagra."

"That's nice," she said, ignoring his authoritarian attitude, but the memory of the article she'd read about his great-great-great-grandfather burst into her mind. Massimo had insisted that he wasn't like his ancestor, but she couldn't help the prickle of fear that skated up her spine. He'd held the woman his son loved prisoner—until she had her baby. Keeping the baby, he'd sent her away. Emma blocked all further thoughts of that article.

Instead, she concentrated on the silver Rolls Royce with the royal crest on the back doors and the two flags on the front fenders, waiting to transport them to the castle. Two black SUVs similar to the ones she saw outside her home were behind the Rolls Royce, and about ten guards stood around the car. She wished he wouldn't be so honorable, but then she wouldn't have come here if she didn't trust his word.

"This is less?" she snickered.

Massimo grinned at her, and sunlight danced over his wavy hair, bringing out blue highlights in the black-as-pitch locks. The baby wore a hat to protect him from the sun, but Emma knew that Steven's thick hair had the same blue highlights.

"In Santino, there wouldn't be any privacy. Only behind the walls of the palace would we have a chance to be normal. But then my mother or my brothers and sister may just drop by."

"Your mother? The queen?"

His men were far enough away that they couldn't hear

their conversation. "She is no longer the reigning queen, but yes, still a queen."

"Of course, that would be Luisa, your bride."

"You're provoking me over a commitment that I must honor based on the law of my country is uncalled for. Tsk, tsk, Emma. Jealousy does not become you."

Emma froze mid-step. "Surely you can't believe I'm envious of her."

Massimo stared at her. "No, perhaps not, but Emma, we certainly will discuss you keeping my son from me." He raised a perfectly shaped black brow before he continued, "How did you feel when you lay in my arms and never once mentioned him to me?"

Emma gasped. "You know my reasons. You promised me you wouldn't mention it again." In a low voice, she added, "I find it rude of you to bring that up now. I've agreed to stay here with you for two weeks. I have nothing else to say to you on that matter." She hurried her steps toward the waiting silver Rolls Royce.

Massimo put the baby in his car seat, and Emma secured him in, then she slid onto the leather seat, and Massimo closed her door before he went around the car to the other side. Nicolo waited for Massimo to get in, then closed his door and proceeded to sit in the front seat next to the driver. The privacy window separating the front and back seats was in use, but Emma didn't want to discuss Steven. And definitely not Luisa, so she gazed out the side window at the beautiful island. *I'm not jealous. He can't be angry that I didn't tell him about Steven. Why did he have to say, I'm the woman of his heart, then cast me aside so he can preserve his honor. He turned his back on me and is marrying someone else. Just like Josh —no, don't go there.*

Wildflowers in a burst of yellows, oranges, and purple colors bordered the road leading up the hillside to the nine-hundred-year-old Romanesque-style stone castle. There were five turrets and a dome in the center of the castle. On the highest point, a red and white flag waved. Emma recognized the design in the center of the flag. It was a replica of the gold medallion Massimo had placed around her neck before he left her that last day in Rome. Elaborate gold iron gates with the king's crest on it parted, and the car drove up the drive. Lush, green manicured lawns bordered the cobblestone drive. They drove through the castle's medieval gate house to an inner courtyard. His driver stopped the car near a red carpet where a line of staff waited for them.

She fought to keep the accusatory tone from her voice. "I thought you said we would be alone."

He grinned, and a glimmer of humor entered his eyes. "We are. Usually when I return home, the number of people to greet me is much more. At the airport in Santino, there would have been a marching band, along with the prime minister and other dignitaries. But here, it's more relaxed. The staff is smaller… under one hundred."

"That small. How will you cope?" Her voice bubbled with suppressed merriment.

"Jest all you want. You will see every person is necessary."

Emma was skeptical. When they exited the car, Massimo again carried Steven. The women curtsied, and the men bowed their heads.

One man, dressed in a black suit, came forward. "Your Majesty, all is ready, as you requested."

"Well done."

Emma stepped into the grand entry with Massimo. She couldn't hold back a gasp. Everything was white marble, from the central staircase to the pillars stretching up. Her eye followed the grandeur of the atrium style entry to the glass dome well above with a view of the sky.

"I'll show you to your rooms, so that you can settle in."

"Do you have a map? This is as huge as your apartment at the palace in Santino."

"Not quite. Although you won't have any issues," Massimo said as he led her down the center of a plush red carpet to a glass and gold elevator. On either side were two carved marble urns filled with fresh flowers. "There are footmen stationed throughout, and everyone speaks English. The castle has all the modern conveniences, including telephones. All you have to do is pick up and someone will be ready to assist you."

They rode the elevator to the third floor. Footmen dressed in red and white uniforms with black knee-high leather boots stood at attention. They walked down a long marble and granite corridor with windows along one side and frescos painted on the walls. The vaulted ceiling was painted in pale blue, with gold moulding. The view of the gardens and sea from the third floor was breathtaking. They reached a set of double elaborate white carved doors trimmed with gilt. Two footmen simultaneously opened both doors for them to enter. The foyer was round and in the center, on a gold table, sat a vase filled with long-stem roses. Pink, similar to the ones he'd given her in Rome. *Don't think of that or the way he ran one velvety soft rose over your naked body—*

"These will be your rooms with your own sitting room... and Steven's nursery is through this connecting door. Let me show you," Massimo said, using his free hand to open the door. "Nicolo and my staff here arranged everything to be set up as you instructed."

"Thank you... And so much more, I see."

He tipped his head, and a slight furrow creased his brow. "I may have added my own suggestions."

The nursery was a masterpiece in pale blue, white, and cream. A crib stood in front of three tall bay windows covered in satin and taffeta drapes. The tie backs were made of the same pale blue silk that adorned the crib. A decorative border of blue pennants circled the room, adding the perfect touch of whimsy. The watercolor wall art in the alcove of jungle animals by a blue velvet accent chair and matching ottoman was ideal to sit in and feed the baby. Near the changing table was a carriage, with big spoke wheels, ready to take Steven for walks.

She turned to Massimo, unable to mask the concern on her face. "When did you do this? You said you only found out about Steven when you spoke to Mr. Collins. When was that? Less than twenty-four hours ago?"

"Yes, that is correct. Emma, the work began in anticipation that I would bond with my son."

Emma slowly shook her head before she walked around the room to the crib. Pale blue silk ties adorned six of the spindles. Running her finger along the railing, she gazed into the crib at the bedding, all cream satin and silk. She thought about what he had said. She opened a door and found the walk-in closet with another dressing table. Tiny baby clothes hung in two tiers across an entire wall. She opened a drawer in the armoire. More clothes were folded neatly and color coordinated. There were bibs in one drawer, rompers and undershirts in another. Kimonos and bath towels. Sweaters and hats with matching booties. The drawers were full of the finest baby clothes. She opened another cabinet and found rows of formula, the brand she'd said that Steven drank, and bottles of water.

She turned to Massimo. Taking a breath, she kept the quiver of fear from her voice. "All of this was prepared while we flew here?"

"Yes, and if there's anything else, you just need to tell me, and it will be gotten."

She lifted Steven from Massimo's arms and walked out of

the dressing room. Laying him on the changing dresser in the nursery, a huge plush giraffe stood next to the table, his head leaning over, that had Steven smiling and kicking his legs. Emma removed his sun hat and lightweight blue knit sweater. Massimo came to stand near them.

"I'm going to try to keep him on his schedule so that we aren't up at three in the morning."

"Very wise. I want to be involved in every step."

"We'll see how you handle a middle of the night feeding, or better yet, a diaper change," Emma said as she prepared to change Steven's diaper. "Will His Majesty, the King do that?"

Massimo laughed. "Probably not, but Maxy can and will."

There it was. Massimo accepted the challenge she threw at him. He would be Maxy, but she knew he really couldn't. He was so much more than that. The absolute ruler of a nation and—far worse than that—he would soon be committed to another woman. Emma pushed those thoughts to the back of her mind as she concentrated on her son.

Once Steven was changed into a clean outfit, Massimo said, "I'll leave you and Steven to settle in." He glanced at his gold wristwatch. "We can have lunch around one o'clock if you like."

"Two would be better. That's his nap time, after I feed him."

"Perfect. I'll see you then." He stroked Steven's head before he kissed him on the cheek, then left the nursery.

Emma caught herself sniffing the air, breathing in Massimo's subtle spicy cologne. She groaned, then concentrated on Steven, cradling him in her arms until he drifted off to sleep. She kissed his brow and laid him in the crib. Picking up the baby monitor, she walked to her room.

Opening a connecting door, her breath caught. "Oh, my God." She stared at an enormous bed with a headboard that was taller than Massimo. The silver-painted wood was covered in carved roses and ribbons. The center of the head-board was tufted silver material, and the matching footboard was a lower replica of the headboard. The bed was made with mountains of lightest cream-colored satin comforters.

A crystal chandelier hung above the bed. A small sitting area with a butter-yellow sofa and two wing chairs in a deeper hue faced the sofa near the fireplace. Sconces added accent lighting on the walls. French doors led to a flagstone terrace.

Emma walked into the dressing room where her meager clothes hung in the tiniest portion of the hanging rods in the enormous room. Someone had arranged her coat and the clothes she'd brought for herself, and placed her shoes on the shoe rack. She changed out of her dress, putting on a pair of shorts and a tank top. She found a fridge in the alcove between her dressing room and the ensuite.

A separate room led to the main entry with a living room and a dining table surrounded by six butter-yellow uphol-stered chairs. Past that, a sitting room. Emma strode to the double French doors leading to her terrace. She stepped out into the glorious sunshine and placed the baby monitor on a low table before she sat on the lounger. Emma gazed out at the aqua water of the Mediterranean Sea. A white sandy beach stretched along the coast like a carpet on the water's edge. Her eyes felt so heavy. This was the first time she had really relaxed since Massimo appeared at her front door. *What have I gotten into? Have I made the right decision to bring Steven here?*

CHAPTER 8

Massimo walked into the nursery. The room was in semi-darkness with the shades lowered. He hadn't mentioned to Emma that the nursery separated his bedroom from hers. This was his apartment, with a living room, a dining room, and a study, and even a small kitchen. She'd been so skittish and nervous, but he realized that her concern was genuine, and that took the edge off some of his anger. It had to do with something in an article she'd read about his great-great-great-grandfather. What she'd read wasn't accurate and just a small part of the story. He wouldn't tell her that this was the very castle where all the drama played out. He pursed his lips. His great-great-grandfather, the crown prince, and his commoner's love story were depicted in frescos leading to the great hall.

He glanced at his wristwatch. It was well past one o'clock, and Steven slept in his crib, a blue knit blanket covering him. Massimo left the nursery through the connecting door into Emma's room. He found her sleeping on a lounger in the hot afternoon sun. *How long has she been sleeping out here?* He scooped Emma up into his arms. Her delicate fair complexion would burn in the sun. He'd seen her in far less, but the short shorts exposed her curvy legs, and the tank top clung to her breasts, accenting her nipples.

Emma sighed. "Mmm." She looped her silky arms around his shoulders and buried her nose in his neck. "Mmmm… Maxy." Her body tensed. She pulled away from him as her eyes flew open. "Put me down. What are you doing? You promised."

"I found you asleep out here. The Malagran sun can be quite strong at this time of year. I was going to lay you on your bed. I have no ulterior motive."

"I can walk," she grumbled.

He slipped his arm from under her knees. Her bare feet touched the floor, and he held her to him for a heartbeat, breathing in her jasmine scent. "Steven is sleeping, but I thought you wanted to feed him."

She glanced at her smart watch. "I can't believe I fell asleep. I forgot to set my alarm."

Just then, Steven cried out over the baby monitor. "He's hungry," Emma said, running her fingers through her luxurious fiery red hair. She pulled a scrunchie from her pocket and gathered her hair up into a messy bun. She hurried into the nursery.

Emma lifted Steven from the crib, cuddling him. She said, in her soft musical voice, "Hello, my darling. You let Mama sleep. You're such a good boy." She turned to Massimo. "Can you hold Steven while I prepare his formula?"

He pressed a button on the wall panel, and the shades covering the windows rose. "Of course," he said, taking the baby from Emma. He brought Steven to the changing table. "I think he needs a new diaper."

"I'll change him before he has his bottle," Emma said.

Massimo handed the baby to her. He went to sit on the ottoman and watched as Emma cooed and talked to Steven.

Once he was in a clean diaper, she sat in the armchair and fed him.

"You are very efficient," he said.

"I won't say lots of practice." She giggled. "But I guess playing with my baby dolls when I was little paid off."

"Ahh, I see." He smiled. "I'll tell Nicolo to have lunch served on the terrace."

"I guess I didn't think this through." Emma put Steven against her shoulder to burp him. "You don't really cook for yourself." She shrugged. "Or… just grab a salad, maybe soup and a sandwich."

He grinned, shaking his head. "No. My chefs, and their staff take care of the cooking. Lunch is usually a minimum of four courses."

"All that food and did I hear right… more than one chef?"

"What can I say? I don't 'grab' fast food or eat at my desk. We don't rush through the day," he teased her, disappointed that Emma ignored him and wouldn't rise to the bait.

"After lunch, I would like to take Steven for a walk in that beautiful baby carriage. I'm probably going to need the exercise."

Massimo picked up the receiver on the telephone next to the chair. "Nicolo, have the midday meal set up on the terrace in Ms. Harris' room."

She rubbed Steven's back. "Before we eat, I'll go change out of these shorts into something more appropriate."

He admired her shapely legs. "You don't need to. Be comfortable.. In Rome, we ate wearing far less."

"That was then." Emma glanced away, but not before he saw her cheeks bloom with a delicate pink blush. She cleared her throat. "Once I put him in his crib, I'll go change."

"Whatever makes you happy. I will be on the terrace." Massimo strolled out through her bedroom to the terrace as his staff set up for lunch. A footman brought him a glass of wine. Massimo stood at the edge of the terrace looking out at the sea. His royal guards in several motorboats crisscrossed the area.

He turned when a footman opened the sliding glass door for Emma.

"This is so beautiful," she said, walking out onto the terrace.

Massimo gazed at her. She'd changed into a blue eyelet, fitted mini dress and gold sandals. *She is the beauty.* "Yes, it is quite lovely," he agreed. Emma had taken her hair out of the bun she wore when holding the baby and her red tresses shimmered around her shoulders in waves reaching almost to her tiny waist. Her natural beauty was unhindered by heavy makeup. Just a hint of coral on her lips—he turned away.

A footman approached with a drink for her. She accepted it, then Massimo led her to the white damask-covered table that was set with his monogrammed china. His personal chef, Francesco, and several servants waited to serve them a delicate and flavorful seafood bisque.

"After our meal, we will take Steven in his pram… or as you say, carriage, down to the gardens."

"Thank you. That would be wonderful."

STEVEN RECLINED IN HIS PRAM, grabbing at the toy she held out to him as Massimo wheeled the carriage through the gardens along a wide path lined with hedges.

"These flowers have such a heavenly scent. The mix of roses, gardenias, and lilies. The vivid colors along the path with the high hedges. I can envision what a secret garden might be like. Do you come here often?"

"I schedule a few visits a year at the castle. Especially

during the summer months when it's nice to get out of the city. I enjoy sailing here and riding my horse in the early morning surf. Do you ride?"

"Yes, some. I know the basics, although I haven't... not in a long time."

They continued their leisurely stroll down the stone path. Steven had fallen asleep while they circled back to the castle. Emma covered a yawn.

"You must be tired. Why don't you have a nap? Dinner is at eight thirty. We can eat at the small dining table in your room."

She smothered another yawn. "I'm sorry. I don't know why I'm so tired. Eight thirty sounds great." They entered the nursery, and she put Steven in his crib. Massimo lowered the shades.

"You go lie down and close your eyes. I'll listen for Steven."

"Okay, thank you, Massimo."

THE FOLLOWING MORNING, Massimo heard Emma's lilting voice as he strolled into the nursery. Sunlight brightened the room, and his gaze turned to where Emma leaned over the crib rail. Barefoot and dressed in whitewashed denim short shorts that hugged her rounded butt, teasing his senses. A yellow tank top outlined her full breasts. His groin stirred at the sight of her.

"Good morning. Did you sleep well your first night in the castle?"

She smiled at him, her red hair in a ponytail that had silky curls cascading down her back. "Yes, and so did Steven. He slept through the night. That's a first for him. Another milestone to record in his baby book."

"Did you bring the book with you? Do you have photographs?"

"Yes, to both. They're in his baby bag. I can show them to you later."

"I would love that. Right now, I've ordered breakfast for you. The staff will bring it to your room."

"Just coffee for me, please. I'm going to give Steven his bath, then feed him before I eat."

Massimo stood next to Emma and leaned over the crib, cooing to his son. Steven squealed and kicked his chubby legs. "He's going to get spoiled with all this attention," Emma said. She lowered the crib rail and lifted Steven. "Bath time in the morning is my favorite time of the day. When I returned to work, I had to give that to his nanny. But on the weekends, I take over. In my exploration of the nursery yesterday, I found the ensuite complete with a child-sized porcelain bathtub with hot and cold running water. He's going to like that. Much better than the plastic tub he has at home."

Massimo walked into the bathing area with Emma. She'd filled the tub and placed the bath recliner in the center. A small red ball floated in the water, along with a plastic blue and white boat and a plastic duck. "Yes, modern plumbing and heating were installed when the castle was completely refurbished."

Their attention was brought back to the baby as Steven played in the water, splashing Emma. She dipped a washcloth into the tub and ran the cloth over Steven. He grabbed at one of the bath toys. "After he drinks his bottle, he'll nap for several hours—probably until lunch. Bath time tuckers him out."

"Lazy boy. Is that so?" Massimo said, and Steven gurgled at him.

Emma laughed. "He's answering you." Then she spoke in a

baby-like voice, "Eat and sleep is all I do, Daddy." Her voice died away. "I'm sorry…that just slipped out."

Massimo stepped closer and gazed into her eyes, the emerald green bright. *I can lose myself in her.* "Of all my many titles, Daddy is the one I'm most proud of." He ruffled Steven's damp hair. "Don't you agree, little man?"

Massimo gazed at Emma as her cheeks became a lovely shade of pink.

"Let's get you dressed and fed," she said, wrapping Steven in a fluffy baby towel. She brought him to the changing table, giving Steven a plush rattle to hold while she put his diaper on. He waved his arms, giggling while she dressed him in a blue cashmere knit romper she'd taken out of his closet earlier.

Emma heated his bottle and went to sit in the oversized blue velvet chair to feed the baby.

Massimo sat on the matching ottoman, watching them. "Will you have dinner with me this evening?"

"Yes, I would like that."

"You don't want to have a nanny, but this castle is large, and it would be difficult to come up here if he cries while we have dinner. I've arranged for a night nurse to be nearby."

"Aren't we going to eat on the terrace or at the dining table in my room?"

"Tonight, yes, but beginning tomorrow evening, we'll eat in one of the smaller dining rooms. It will be a pleasant change."

"I've never left him with a stranger."

"My staff has the utmost discretion. I told Nicolo to find someone with both nanny and medical training. Steven will be well cared for."

"I just meant…I don't know the person. At home, I interviewed over twenty nannies from three different agencies before I chose the one I hired."

Emma looked so serious. All he wanted was to strip her clothes from her perfect curves before he carried her over to the nearest wall to drive himself deep into her heat—until she begged him to never stop.

He nodded. "I'll call Nicolo, and we can meet the nanny after breakfast. You can interview her, and we can make a final decision."

"That sounds reasonable, thank you. Later this afternoon, I would like to take Steven for a walk in the garden."

"I wouldn't miss that."

She smiled at him, and his day brightened with thoughts of her. "Let's go have breakfast."

"I'll get his baby book and meet you."

After they finished eating, Emma curled up on the double lounger with the baby book on her lap. The cover was designed with blue and yellow blocks, and each one contained a letter spelling out his name. Massimo sat next to her, itching to put his arm around her shoulder. Earlier, when Steven had splashed while playing in the tub, the thin material of her yellow top had gotten damp. She didn't realize how the fabric clung to her breasts. He fought the urge to tug her into his arms, lift the top, and bury his face between her breasts before teasing the nipples into hard peaks.

"Here, this was taken at my baby shower," she said, handing him a photo.

He held the snapshot of Emma. Her creamy complexion projected an inner glow. She was wearing a blue dress, and her long red hair cascaded in lustrous, loose curls around her shoulders. She was smiling, and her delicate hands outlined her stomach in a profile view. The caption read, *Nine months and waiting*. Massimo gazed at Emma. "Were you alone when you gave birth to him?"

"No—I wanted to work as long as I could, so that I would

have more leave once he was born. I was at the office. It was around four in the afternoon when I felt the first sharp pain. I thought I'd have time to go home." She gazed up at him and shook her head. "That was a mix of naivete and oh, no, this can't be happening now." Emma covered a giggle with her hand. "Mrs. Collins was visiting her husband, and she took one look at me and insisted on driving me straight to the hospital. I called the doctor, then my father. My aunt drove in from Connecticut and met us at the hospital. Steven was born ten hours later." *I missed this.*

"Did you know you were having a boy?"

A flash of humor lit her face. "Yes, I'm a planner, and I needed to know so that I could decorate and have everything ready."

His brow rose. "The spontaneous woman from Rome?"

A delightful, rosy blush ignited her cheeks, and her musical laugh filled the air. "That was different. You took my breath away," she said before shifting her emerald-green gaze away from him. She leaned forward, turned a page in the book, and pointed to a tiny form in the photo. "This is my first ultrasound…see? That's him."

"I'm sorry you went through this alone. Had I known, I would have been there for you."

"Thank you for saying that. My aunt, my mother's sister, stayed with us until Steven was a month old."

"It's good that you had family with you, and now, you have me, too." They still had a lot to discuss, especially about her keeping his son hidden from him, but at least she wasn't arguing with him or purposely getting him upset with the mention of Luisa. "I'm curious. What about your mother? Was she there?"

"She died when I was in elementary school."

"I'm sorry. It's never easy losing a parent," he said.

"How old were you when that happened?"

"I was twenty-five when my father died after a sudden illness. Once he was diagnosed, we both knew I would ascend the throne sooner than later. He was a good king, and his compassion knew no bounds. We spent many hours talking, and his advice and guidance have been the basis for my reign. The mantle, at times, can weigh heavy. The privilege of leading a nation is filled with traditions, duty, and honor. One of the last things he said to me was never forget you are there to serve for the good of all. And so now, I have come to the end of my speech."

She giggled at that. "I had no idea you carried around a soapbox."

He liked her easy banter and had missed that from their brief time in Rome. Massimo slipped his phone from his pocket and called Nicolo, who escorted the nanny to the living room so that Emma could interview her. Nicolo introduced Bianca, an older woman with streaks of gray mixed in her chocolate-brown hair. Her brown eyes were warm and inviting. She'd retired to Isola del Sole from the mainland of Malagra. Bianca curtsied. "Your Majesty," she said when Nicolo introduced her.

"Nicolo, I'll ring when we are finished."

"Yes, Your Majesty," he said and left the room.

He invited Bianca to sit on the sofa while Emma asked questions about her qualifications. "I'm impressed. The agency is well known in the US as well. You can begin this evening. I will have Nicolo show you to your quarters. Once you're settled, you can meet Steven."

"Thank you, Your Majesty, Ms. Harris."

When the nanny left, Emma said, "Seeing that we really wouldn't leave the grounds of the castle, Bianca will work out."

Mid-afternoon, Emma put Steven in his carriage. He played with a toy while they went down to the gardens along the back of the castle. Past the manicured shrubs and lawns, there was a path with a beautiful view of the Mediterranean. The sea was calm today and looked like a sheet of aqua glass. Massimo led her to a walking bridge, and they crossed over a stream of gurgling water. She stopped on the wooden bridge. "No moat? This is definitely a nice added surprise."

CHAPTER 9

Massimo breathed in her jasmine scent before he whispered close to her ear, "Red, I have a castle with a moat. It was built well over a thousand years ago to defend Malagra."

She looked beautiful as she turned to him, her green eyes wide in surprise. "Seriously?"

"One day, I will take you there. You know, I have never lied to you."

Emma blinked, and her long, dark lashes brushed her cheeks before she said, "That's true. Even in Rome, when I asked if you would be my knight in shining armor, you said that you left your armor at the palace. Naturally, I thought you were playing along. When I did come to the palace, I saw that you really did have armor. It was true and not an omission."

Massimo pounced on the opportunity. "Now, there is a word. Omission, the same as you omitted you had a baby, and I was the father." He couldn't stop the anger that seeped into his voice.

She lifted her chin. "I don't want to talk about that. When

I found out who you were, I was eager to tell you. I'd found you, the man who I couldn't stop thinking of. The man whose baby I had. Then I read that article talking about… well you know what I read."

"That is not an excuse for keeping my son from me."

He heard her deep intake of breath. Gazing at the beauty of her face, her cheeks filled with blotches of color. Emma opened her mouth to argue with him—no one but she would dare that.

"Before you say anything else, let me tell you that you don't know the full story. Let's sit over there on the bench." The only sound was that of the pram's wheels as they walked across the wooden bridge to a secluded area. Natural stone chalice urns filled with an assortment of pink and white blooming plants stood on either side of the wrought-iron bench.

Steven had fallen asleep. Emma adjusted him in the pram, raising the hood, then covering him with a light blanket. She sat down next to him.

"I will tell you, my great-great-great-grandfather was a tyrant. He had five daughters and only one son. His son, the crown prince, met and fell in love with a commoner. They were madly in love, and the prince was going to marry her, but his father, the king, wouldn't hear of it, and he sent her away. The king had other plans. He wanted to form an alliance with the neighboring kingdom. It had vast lands, but a weak ruler. The crown prince found out what his father was up to. The plan was advantageous for Malagra, although he wouldn't be dangled like a carrot. The prince loved his commoner more than the king's plan. The king was determined and stole her from her home, but before he could banish her from Malagra, the prince stepped in, taking her away. It wasn't against her will. She loved her prince very much and would do anything to be with him.

This is the very castle that he brought her to. He hid her here."

Emma lifted her head and looked at him, her eyes rounded.

"Let me finish. I know it sounds bad, but as I said, she loved him. She and the crown prince had a child. The king was furious. He would banish the woman and take her child, but the crown prince told his father that he would renounce the throne and take her and his child from Malagra. My ancestor, the king, was shrewd. He knew his son would follow through on his threat, so he agreed that his son could marry the commoner, and the child would become king one day. My ancestor had to placate the other kingdom and avoid a war. His own son almost foiled his ultimate goal to join the two kingdoms and become the ruler of both. He found a way to have everything he wanted, so he offered his eldest daughter in marriage and passed a law that from that point on, all future kings of Malagra would have to marry a woman of royal blood. There would be no exceptions. So here I am, prepared to marry a woman I don't love. I will give up on my happiness for my country."

"I must admit that I stopped reading after the part where the king took her baby."

"Yes, it was ruthless how he tried to control the crown prince and definitely not what I want. You know Steven is safe."

Emma's soft hand lay on his thigh, burning him as she said, "Maxy, I am sorry that I didn't tell you. I was so worried and not sure what you would do. When you summoned me to the palace, I couldn't help myself. I wanted to be with you for at least a few hours." She moved her hand and shrugged. "You had made it very clear to me that nothing other than sex could be between us."

"I never lied to you. From the beginning, I was honest with you."

She nodded. "I know, but it still hurt."

"You do know that I am living in my own hell." Massimo stood. "Let's walk around this way." They continued along the path to a secluded area of the garden. The sun peeked through the tall shade trees as they talked. "I want to show you the fresco depicting their love story when we get back in the castle." They arrived at an inner courtyard, and he led the way into the castle to the great hall. On the walls, the high arched gilt ceilings, the frescos of his ancestor, and the woman he would have given everything up for. "You know they made this castle their home, raising a family here until he ascended the throne as king, and she was his queen. After he became king, he moved into the palace on Santino."

"I had not realized that."

They brought Steven to the nursery and laid him in his crib so that he could continue his nap. Massimo went to his office. He needed to think about what Emma had said. She wanted one more night with him. Didn't he feel the same way about her? His heart thudded. Needing her had become a physical pain. He'd fought the urge to find her in the year since Rome. Honor, obligations, duty, and his commitment to serve his country prevented him. His great-great-grandfather, when he was crown prince, stood up to his father for the woman he loved.

Massimo strode to the window, looking out over the gardens. He wouldn't turn his back on his country, no matter his feelings for Emma. He would go through with his intention of marrying Luisa. Could he keep Emma here? Would she willingly stay with him?

CHAPTER 10

When Massimo left, Emma picked up the book she'd been reading and sat on the butter-yellow chaise lounge in her bedroom. The words on the page dimmed as she thought about what Massimo had said. How he'd given up on his happiness for the love of his country.

Emma snapped her book closed. "Well, I was dragged into this, and what about Lady Luisa?" She stood and paced the room, then glanced at her smart watch. Steven would be up soon and ready to eat. She didn't want to think about anything else. Even if she'd told Massimo about Steven right away, he couldn't marry her. She shrugged. *So what if he accused me of being jealous, or that he said he couldn't trust me? None of it mattered.* She ran her fingers through her hair. *He's bound by his oath to his country and the throne to marry—not me —stop making yourself sick over this. It can't change anything.*

She walked to the terrace doors, looking through the arched floor-to-ceiling clear glass. Her thoughts were spinning. How would she be emotionally once he *did* marry Lady Luisa? There'd be no place on earth where she could escape. When Josh had married his Emma, it had hurt for a while, but she'd eventually forgotten about him and moved on with her life. Forgetting Massimo would be so very difficult. How could she force herself not to think of Massimo and Lady Luisa? Was there a way to give herself amnesia?

Steven cried out, and Emma put those thoughts out of her mind as she walked to the nursery. Massimo had already arrived and was holding Steven in his arms. "I was nearby waiting for him to wake up," he said before he flashed one of his kryptonite smiles at her. "Why don't I change him while you prepare his bottle?"

"Sure." She stepped away to mix formula and water for Steven. She hid her misting eyes from him. *I guess it will be good practice for when he and Lady Luisa start their family.*

"Tonight, we will have dinner on your terrace at eight-thirty."

AT THE PRECISE TIME, Massimo knocked on her bedroom door. He wore a dark vest with matching pants and a white shirt open at the collar. *No suit jacket. This must be casual for him.* Emma wore one of the last dresses she'd brought with her. She'd packed hastily and realized that she'd chosen mostly jeans and shorts, her yoga pants, a belly top, and a bunch of tank tops rather than fancy.

Luckily, it was dinner on the terrace of her room, and the blue dress was pretty enough—although the terrace felt like a five-star restaurant with servers and his chef in attendance. They dined on the most delicate flavorful salmon she'd ever eaten. Emma sipped at her wine until the staff brought out dessert, along with espresso. "I'm stuffed." She leaned forward and whispered, "Do you eat like this all the time?" She placed her linen napkin on the table.

Massimo grinned before he stood. Taking her hand, they

walked to the edge of the stone terrace, gazing out over the gardens to the view of the beach below. The air was perfumed with the scent of flowers. A slight breeze ruffled his hair, and Emma couldn't help breathing in the scent of his intoxicating cologne.

A server carried a silver tray with two brandy glasses. Massimo handed her one of the crystal tumblers before he took his.

Massimo leaned his hip against the Mediterranean-style stone railing. "Where do you eat?"

"Me? If my father is there, then we eat together, in the breakfast nook. When he's at work… sometimes it's a sandwich in front of the TV. I'm too exhausted for more than that when I get home from the office. Steven's nanny has nights off, so I usually bring him into the living room. He stays in his swing and…" Emma tipped her head to the side, smiling before she added, "he watches TV with me."

"I don't have any memories of sharing meals with my parents." His voice sounded distant. "I ate alone, then with my younger brothers and sister. It was the same for them. Our nannies took care of us most of the time. When I was old enough to go to boarding school, I ate with my classmates in the dining hall."

Emma stopped herself from reaching out, instead taking another sip of the delicious amber liquid. "That is certainly different. We always ate together… even after my mother died. My father changed his schedule and worked during the day so that we would be together in the evenings."

Massimo kissed her brow. "Our son is lucky that you're his mother."

Warmth spread through her at his praise.

"It's late. I will see you in the morning," he said and left.

. . .

THE NEXT MORNING Emma gazed at Massimo as he lay on the pale blue-and-cream Persian rug in the middle of the nursery. He looked like a supermodel in a navy-blue polo shirt that molded to every part of his broad shoulders and down his ripped torso. The muscles in his forearm moved as he held a red ball between his long, tanned fingers to Steven. She watched them from the velvet armchair as the baby lay in his bouncy seat, reaching for the toy. Massimo's faded jeans clung to his long, muscular legs all the way to his narrow hips. She had to turn away.

The ache for him had begun again, or had it ever stopped? She squashed it and her desire for a man she could never have. Her sexual attraction to Massimo was almost out of control. With a simple look from his captivating blue eyes, she would gladly fall into his bed. His words about how much he had to give up for his country played on an endless loop in her head.

Emma prepared Steven's bottle before she picked him up and brought him to sit in the overstuffed armchair. She placed a cotton blue and white bib embroidered with yellow ducks on it around Steven's neck. Cradling her baby in the crook of her arm, she gave him his bottle.

"This is my favorite time of day. Sitting with you while you feed our son his morning meal." Massimo's deep voice was filled with awe.

"Me too. I like how you start your day with us. You said this is your retreat, but I see that you actually do work from here."

"Today, I have completely cleared my calendar. I have nothing but time for us. No phone calls or interruptions. I have read all the updates I needed to read. I want to take you and Steven to the beach."

"We have to find shade for him. Perhaps if we go early, before the sun becomes too strong?"

"Last night when you mentioned a swing, it gave me the idea to have one delivered. It will be perfect. The frame has a hood that we can use for shade to protect him from the sun."

"Then that sounds like fun." Steven finished his bottle, and Emma put her son on her shoulder to rub his back. "Once he burps, we can eat… I'm starving."

"I will be right back," he said. Rising from the floor to his full six-foot-two height, he turned and sauntered out of the nursery toward his room. She couldn't help admiring his body… the way he filled his jeans.

A moment later, Massimo returned with two gift boxes, one wrapped in blue paper and the other in gold foil. He frowned. "He fell asleep? That was quick," he said with a chuckle.

"Yes, a clean diaper, fed, and burped. He's good for a few hours," she said, laying Steven in his crib. "What are those?" she whispered.

"The larger is for you, and the smaller is for Steven." Massimo handed her the gifts, then grabbed the oval baby monitor before they walked into her room. Emma sat on the sofa and first opened Steven's gift. Moving the delicate blue tissue paper, she revealed a tiny pair of baby swim trunks and a coverup. Tucked in a corner was a big floppy beach hat and a pair of baby sunglasses. "Oh, Maxy, this is so cute and thoughtful of you. Thank you." In her excitement, she had called him Maxy.

"Open yours." His smile dazzled her. She lifted the lid on her gift box. Between the folds of the most exquisite silver tissue paper, she found a red bikini bathing suit. "I… thank you. I hadn't thought to pack a swimsuit."

"I asked your lady's maid." He shrugged a broad shoulder. "While we are at the beach, a few more clothes will be delivered for you, including a riding outfit."

She gazed at him. "Massimo, I can't—"

"Humor me…didn't you say you were starving? Let's go eat."

She nodded, leaving the gifts on the cushion of the butter-yellow sofa.

Morning sunlight bathed the terrace, and the outdoor table sparkled with crystal glasses, red china plates, cups with saucers, and sterling-silver flatware. His monogram graced all the china. Would she ever get used to all the staff that waited on His Majesty, the King?

This morning, she had dressed in one of the two sundresses she'd packed. Most of her wardrobe was business attire. She didn't have very many casual clothes. Her maternity clothes had been economically chosen and were too big for her to wear. Besides, they were inappropriate for this setting.

Massimo waved the footman away and held her seat for her to sit. Then he went to his seat and allowed the footman to pull out his chair. Once their food was served, the staff moved away, giving them privacy. "I have told Nicolo to prepare an area for us on the beach."

Curiosity won, and Emma lowered her voice. "Nicolo does so much. Was he in Rome with you?"

He nodded. "Yes, along with my bodyguards, my three valets, and my chef. The flight crew stayed on my plane."

Emma stared into his blue eyes. "I'm amazed that I didn't see any of your entourage."

His right brow rose. "They are trained to melt into the background." He took a last sip of his coffee before a footman approached to slide his chair backward for him. "Come," he said.

The touch of his hand as he took her elbow penetrated her thoughts, filling her with desire as he led her into her room and away from his people. They sat on the sofa. "Our time in Rome was brief, and I wanted to keep you all to myself."

"Were they near when we went out?"

"Yes, my guards are always with me. Emma, we shared a wonderful seventy-two hours. I never lied to you. I wanted so much to tell you who I was. You were so open, and I loved that you were carefree. Everything I couldn't be." He compelled her to gaze into his blue eyes. "The first time you called me Maxy..." He leaned in, and his spicy scent enveloped her. "I never had a nickname before. You made me feel normal. I will say that normalcy is something I could never really have. You've made me wish for that, which is impossibly out of reach."

"Massimo, we packed so much into that short time. In the days and weeks after I returned home... I couldn't forget you. Then when I realized I was expecting your baby... to be fair, I really tried to find out who you were. I called the hotel, but their policy of discretion wouldn't permit them to give me any information. They wouldn't forward a letter to you. They refused, saying that would defeat their policy of anonymity. I attempted to locate you by searching the internet for the medallion you gave me. It was futile. I can see now that your signet ring is a miniature of it."

He moved his hand. "Yes, my guards insisted I not wear the ring, only the medallion hidden under my shirt for security purposes."

"I guess that makes sense."

He grinned. "Tell me more about when you found out who I was."

Emma shifted her gaze, realizing that he didn't ask out of vanity but that he was genuinely curious. "By that time, I'd returned to work after my maternity leave. Steven was three months old. I wanted to tell you that very day. Then once I read about you on the internet, how this was an absolute monarchy, I became concerned that you might take Steven from me. I didn't know what to do. I had to work on the project. Now that I was a single mother, I couldn't chance putting my position with the company in jeopardy. Mr. Collins has always been kind to me and very understanding. He offered to pay for Steven and his nanny to come with me. I was too worried that if you found out about him…well, I left Steven at home with my father and the nanny. There was a lot of doubt and anxiety going on at the time…" She tipped her head to one side. "Possibly hormones as well."

"Yes, there is that."

When she next spoke, her voice was full of entreaty. "You said you couldn't trust me… but I… I did feel guilty after we made love, and I didn't tell you about Steven. While I was in your arms, all I thought about was savoring every moment of our time together. I couldn't help myself. If there were a way to memorize you, I would have. I wanted to hold on to your memory forever…" She bowed her head and stared at his long fingers with their perfectly manicured nails.

Massimo reached under her chin, and she gazed into his eyes, surrounded by thick, long lashes. He took her hands. "No, Emma. I was angry, but you're here now." He kissed her fingers. "Shall we prepare to go down to the beach?" he asked before standing.

She nodded. "Yes. I'll get ready. By then, Steven should be up, and I can change him."

CHAPTER 11

*E*mma walked beside Massimo as he led her down a secluded path barely wider than the pram he pushed until it opened up and spread out onto a white sandy beach. She'd expected a beach umbrella and two chairs, but nothing was that simple when His Majesty, King Massimo, was involved.

They reached a cabana covered in red-and-white striped canvas, complete with a gold pennant that fluttered in the sea breeze. The front of the cabana faced the water, with sheer white curtains tied back. An outdoor couch and table sat under the tent. A carpet spread out in front of that, with Steven's swing on it. Past that, a blanket had been laid over the white sand. The sound of the waves gently lapping at the shore and the briny scent of the Mediterranean Sea were something Emma would always remember.

"This is so beautiful and peaceful. I can see why you would want to come here for downtime."

Massimo reclined on his side, resting on an elbow. His aqua swim trunks hugged his narrow waist and covered his upper thighs. A breeze ruffled his black hair, and Emma wanted to reach over and smooth the disobedient lock back from his brow. At the moment, he was moving a wooden tile on the game board to make a word.

Emma lay on her stomach, her knees bent, and her ankles crossed. She was excited to place her tiles down. "Maxy, you said only French words, but I honestly don't think that is a word in any language."

"Of course it is," he replied in his husky voice.

"I'll need proof," she said, reaching for her phone.

"If I am correct, you will forfeit five points." He smiled at her.

She laughed at that. "I'll take my chances."

She slid her phone over and typed in the five letters he'd placed on the board. MEUGLE. "Moo, you spelled MOO. The sound a cow makes."

A smile spread across his sexy lips. He leaned forward.

Her throat dried, she couldn't breathe, and her lips parted.

"I win," he said.

The sky looks washed out in comparison to the vibrancy in his eyes. Heat sizzled in her core, then her body stiffened. Astonished by her reaction, she scrambled to her feet.

Massimo stood. "Steven's playing with the toys that we strung across his swing. I'm going to dip his toes in the surf." He lifted the baby from the swing and headed to the water.

Emma hurried after him. "Oh, do you think that's a good idea?" She couldn't hide the concern in her voice. "I read that no bathing in the ocean or pools before six months."

"Dipping only his toes for less than thirty seconds. He's going to love it." Massimo stopped and lifted him up over his head. "What do you think?" Steven laughed, kicking his feet. "See, he's all excited," he said to Emma. He balanced Steven face down across his forearm, swooshing him around like an airplane.

"Wait, let me put more sunblock on him."

Massimo turned to her, his bare chest covered with a smattering of black hair, his washboard abs covered with a sheen of sunblock. His swim trunks rode low on his narrow hips. The muscles in his thighs moved as he walked.

"Emma, if you apply any more of that to him, he'll probably slip right out of my arms."

Emma's eyes widened and she couldn't respond.

He chuckled. "I promise not to drop our son."

Our son, our son. Joy overwhelmed her. "Oh you, for a moment… I… well, thought you were serious. let me grab my phone so I can take a picture."

"No photos of me in my swim trunks and none of Steven's face."

"What? Why not?" Emma walked beside Massimo as he continued to the water's edge. He turned to her. "I do not want to see us on social media."

"Oh." She pretended to pout before she said, "I was ready to hashtag you and post them to all my accounts. Probably make a video too."

The sun turned his bronzed skin golden, and the grin on his handsome chiseled features almost buckled her knees.

"I wanted to send some to my father, so he can see how we're doing."

"Okay, you may do that but be sure to let him know not to post any of them."

She laughed. "He barely can reply to a text message."

Massimo crouched down on his haunches while he held Steven upright, making sure to not let his feet touch the hot sand, only the cool, packed sand where the water lapped at the shore. Emma went further into the warm water so she could get in front of them and snap some photos with her phone.

"Oh Maxy, he's enjoying this so much. Later, I'll text my dad."

"I'm sure your father will like that."

"Give me your phone, and you hold him." Massimo took a few pictures of her with Steven, then he stood next to them, his arm around her shoulder. He took a selfie. "You can add this to his baby book under the heading, Daddy, Mommy and me—first day at the beach and first time in the Mediterranean."

They walked to the cabana. The Scrabble board had been cleared away, and the blanket smoothed.

"We should go back to the castle before midday, when the sun is at its strongest," he said.

Emma held Steven and was going to lay him in the pram when Massimo said, "I'll hold him. One of the staff will bring the pram back to the castle."

After their fun-filled morning, Emma gave Steven a quick bath to remove the sunblock, then put him in fresh diaper and laid him in his crib. Massimo had gone to change for lunch. When Emma walked into her room, she found her lady's maid hanging her clothes in the dressing room. "Hello, Miss Harris. These arrived. I was preparing them for you."

"All of this?" Emma stepped further inside. Her meager clothes had been pushed to the side, along with her coat. The racks were now packed with an assortment of clothing, from casual to fancy ballgowns. Shoes in every style and heel height, from flats to stiletto, lined the shoe racks. She opened a drawer filled with lacy bras and in the drawer below, matching thongs and panties. Frilly nightgowns and silk robes hung on the racks above them. "Shall I draw you a bath and choose something for you to wear?" *What's his purpose? Buy me with this? Just because he changes four times a day is no reason for me to, and we go home in less than two weeks.*

"I'm going to shower and..." She skimmed a rack of

casual dresses. "I'll wear this one for lunch," she said, taking a mint-green, short-sleeve, fit-and-flare dress off the hanger and held it to her.

"Very nice choice, Miss Harris. That color brings out the emerald green in your eyes."

~

LATER THAT AFTERNOON, when she and Massimo had finished lunch, Emma said, "Do you even know where the kitchen is?"

He pursed his sculpted lips and frowned, bringing out the dimple in his chin. "Why would I need to know that? Francesco comes to me, or I tell Nicolo what it is I wish for a meal."

"I guess that makes sense since you don't know what the best takeout-slash-takeaway food is."

He lifted a black brow, and she covered a giggle behind her hand at the look on his handsome face.

"Really, Ms. Harris. I suppose you can cook."

"Yes, and bake too. I make a mean chocolate chip cookie. It's one of my happiest memories with my mother."

He slipped his phone from his pocket, touched his finger to the screen, and spoke into it to send a voice-to-text message. "Nicolo, have the chef come up to my apartment immediately." Ending the call, he put his phone back into his pocket. "There is a smaller kitchen here on this floor. See, I know some things. You tell Francesco what you need to make cookies, and he will provide it."

Before he finished, there was a knock at the living room door, and one of his uniformed guards let in his very frazzled chef. He wore a spotlessly clean chef's jacket and black pants. "Your Majesty," he said as he bowed. "Was the meal not to your liking?"

"No, Francesco, the meal was superb as always. Ms.

Harris will tell you what she needs for now. Later, I want you to stock the smaller kitchen."

"*Si*, Your Majesty, immediately," he said.

Emma told the chef what she needed, then he bowed again to Massimo before hurrying from the living room. "Poor Francesco. He was beside himself. He didn't know what he could do to please you."

"Francesco is a good man. He's been with me for a very long time. All I want, Red, is to make you happy."

"No, you just want a chocolate chip cookie," she said, smiling at him.

Less than fifteen minutes later, Massimo's phone rang. "Yes," he said. "Good work, Nicolo." Turning to her, he said, "The kitchen is stocked." He lifted the white oval baby monitor. "If he cries, we will hear him."

"The beach tuckered him out. I'm amazed at how quickly your request was met. Are you going to help me?"

"Of course, Red. I will be your sous chef."

"Oh, really? This will be very interesting. His Majesty as an assistant."

His eyes held a hint of amusement. "Another first for me."

She liked the easy banter that had begun last night and continued this morning at the beach. Nothing in the castle was small, including the long carpet-covered hallway at the back of the apartment. They strolled, their steps in sync, until they reached white wood-carved doors that opened into the kitchen.

"This kitchen is as large as the entire first floor of my house," Emma said. Crystal chandeliers hung from the tray ceiling. One large focal point in the center and a similar smaller one at the sink and each of the work areas. Warm-toned wood cabinets lined two walls. Wood floors in the exact color of the cabinets stretched across the entire space. The countertops were a work of art, with silver veins running through the white marble. The appliances were top-of-the-line stainless steel.

"Yes, but for the castle, it is small. The main galley is much larger, with a separate pastry kitchen." Massimo was true to his word. Rolling up the sleeves of his button-down silk shirt, he helped her measure out the flour and softened the butter once she showed him how to use the microwave. The scent of vanilla and brown sugar wafted around them. Emma did a quick calculation from Fahrenheit to Celsius, broke the eggs she needed, and mixed the ingredients. "You're very precise. I can see the engineer in you. Was it always your desire to build?"

"Funny you say that. Naturally, I played with dolls when I was little and dreamed of being a princess for sure. After my mother died, my father thought we should have a hobby that we could share. At first, it was jigsaw puzzles, and that was great. Then, one day, he brought home building blocks. Of course, I wanted to build a castle. The walls kept falling. He said I needed a firm foundation, but more than that, the ground had to be solid."

"Is your father an engineer?"

"No, at the time, he was a firefighter. Now, he's the chief."

"Interesting."

The smell of cookies filled the space, and Emma removed the final tray from the oven. While they cooled, she placed the first batch on a plate, then went to the refrigerator. "The best way to eat these is with a glass of ice-cold milk for dunking," she said, carrying a crystal pitcher of milk to the counter.

His brow furrowed.

"Kings don't dunk?" she asked, suppressing a giggle.

He strolled to the counter, placed two glasses next to the cookies, and stood close to her. His vibrant blue eyes sparked with a mix of amusement and something else Emma couldn't decipher. "I'll make an exception."

"What about you? Did you have childhood dreams?" Emma sounded breathless and tried to calm her racing heart.

"Growing up? I may have wanted to be a police officer, or a helicopter pilot would have been fun. As I grew older, I understood that one day I would be king, so there wasn't much opportunity for anything else. When I turned eighteen, my father told me that someday I would head the government and the military." He shrugged a broad shoulder. "So, after three years of service, one year in each branch, I went to law school, followed by a master's degree in political science and another year in Parliament, learning the ins and outs of the government. To lead as monarch is so much more than traditions and ceremony. I was bound by commitment and duty to serve my country. I thought I would have more time to settle into my obligations, but my father took ill... then, as they say, the rest is history."

"You are in the history books. In preparation for the hospital project, I read how you've brought top-of-the-line health care to all the people of Malagra. The minister of urban development sang your praises."

"My cousin Gino? Yes."

"Oh, I hadn't realized he was family. Once he learned you were coming to see the model of the hospital, he and his staff gave my team a quick lesson in protocol. He even taught the women how to curtsy and the proper way the men should bow their heads."

"It's an honor and at times, a burden—"

The baby monitor interrupted as Steven cried out.

Emma glanced at her wristwatch before nodding. "Right on schedule. He has an inner timer that is better than the world clock."

Massimo's voice was full of mirth. "I have noticed that about our son."

They left the kitchen and walked to the nursery. Emma lifted Steven from his crib and went to the changing table.

"Steven had a busy morning at the beach. Can we watch a movie rather than go for our afternoon walk?"

"Yes, I'll have the theater set up—"

Turning her head, she lifted a brow. "The theater... of course you have one... but how about in the living room?"

"I think we can manage that." He slid his phone from his pocket. "Is there anything in particular you wish to see?"

"A drama might be nice," she said.

"I know just the one. I will call Nicolo."

CHAPTER 12

$\mathcal{I}$n the few short days since Massimo had brought her to the medieval castle by the sea, they'd fallen into a comfortable routine. Mornings were spent with the baby, then while he napped, she and Massimo would share breakfast. After that, a walk in the gardens or the beach. Emma didn't think about his royal status. He was just Maxy, and Lady Luisa was forgotten.

"Tomorrow, we can have dinner on the beach, just you and me."

"I love the beach. At home, I don't get to go nearly as often as I like. Besides, the summers are too short."

"Isola del Sole is so far south, it boasts of a mild climate all year round."

The following evening, at the expected knock, Emma gave herself one last look in the mirror and patted her hair before she opened the door. Massimo stood there in a dark suit with a crisp white silk shirt, open at the collar. A smile spread across his sculpted lips. She couldn't take a breath as his gaze traveled from her face, down her body. Her breasts burned when his blue eyes lingered before moving down to her sandal-covered feet and back up to gaze into her eyes. "You look beautiful," he said in a deep voice.

The silver slip dress she'd chosen offered no protection, and her pulse skipped a beat before it raced at the desire his smoldering eyes ignited in her core. Her voice quivered. "Thank you. You look quite dashing."

His bergamot-infused cologne drifted around her. He smiled, and her belly did a flip. *Oh God, Emma, is it wise to be alone with him?*

Massimo led her out of the castle. The dim glow from the landscape lights lit the way along a stone path and down the worn stone steps to the beach. Silver moonbeams cast a glow over a carpet that spread across the sand.

Emma stopped. "This isn't a blanket on the beach. It's much fancier even than the cabana the other day."

The square, intimate table was covered in a billowing cloth brushing the carpet. Tall candelabras stood near each corner, their flames flickering and dancing in the night. Men and women in black suits with red vests—the uniform of his wait staff—waited as they prepared to serve their meal. Guards in black suits were positioned at intervals along the water's edge.

Massimo's hand touched the small of her back. "No, certainly not a simple blanket," he said, guiding her to one of the two high-back red velvet chairs. "After dinner, we'll walk along the beach."

She lowered her voice. "This is not a date nor—"

"I get it, Red." His husky whisper sizzled through her body.

She drew in a shaky breath. *The warning is more for me.* All he had to do was nudge her, and she would gladly fall into his bed.

Massimo waved the footman away and held out her chair before he walked to his, where a footman stepped forward to assist him. He nodded to his chef. A sterling-silver dome-covered china plate was placed before each of them.

"Hot dogs?" she teased.

"You think I've never eaten a hot dog? On a visit to New York City, I had one." His brow furrowed. "What are they made of?"

"It's not wise to ask."

He nodded. "What I did like were the huge warm pretzels from—what are they called?"

"Street vendors."

A server filled their crystal glasses with white wine. Massimo's long finger skated around the rim. "Tonight, we're having lobster."

Across the intimate table, his husky voice flooded Emma with warmth. Their easy banter and his sexy smile reminded her of Rome.

The sonorous sound of violins filled the briny evening air. Emma savored the delicate flavor of lobster and buttery sauce, as much as she wanted to savor this time with him. *Why do I torment myself?*

It was impossible to drag her eyes away from Massimo's chiseled features, his powerful neck with a few chest hairs teasing her. She admired how his broad shoulders filled his dark custom-made jacket.

With the last bite of the entrée, a footman removed their plates. "I hope you saved room for dessert. I remember your delight with the chocolate hazelnut cake we shared in Rome."

"Oh, that was the best dessert." She loved that he remembered how much she'd enjoyed that cake. "You called it *la petite morte,* by chocolate."

A hint of a smile touched his sensuous lips. His pastry

chef came forward. "Your Majesty, the dessert you requested." Two footmen followed, each holding a gold fluted-edge
plate with a slice of fudgy hazelnut cake slathered with
chocolate ganache. They placed the plates before them.

Emma dipped her fork into the slice and brought it to her
lips. The taste of the decadent dessert lingered on her
tongue. She closed her eyes and held back a moan, savoring
the taste. *Oh.* Her stomach tensed. She put her fork down as
the memory of them sharing a piece of the rich dessert in his
suite in Rome assailed her. Then, she hadn't held back her
delight. He'd flashed a sexy smile and said in his husky
accented voice, "Red, you make the same sounds when I'm
deep in you, making you come. Let me show you."

Now, his gaze held hers across the flickering candles at
the intimate table. She twisted the linen napkin on her lap
between her fingers, feeling the heat rise into her cheeks. *Is
he thinking about what happened next? Oh God, he lifted me onto
the dining table and—*Her heart fluttered.

Massimo brought his demitasse cup to his lips and drank
his espresso in one shot. Placing the cup back on its saucer,
the violin music stopped. For a moment, only the surf broke
the silence of the night.

He stood and held out his hand. "Dance with me?"

She gazed at him. "Here, right now?"

"Yes."

Emma placed the tips of her fingers in his outstretched,
warm hand before she stood. His long fingers closed over her
hand. She curtsied as the violinists began a waltz. Massimo
slid his powerful arm around her waist and tugged her
against his hard body. He led her in the steps of the slow,
sensuous dance. She breathed in his spicy scent, the smooth
soft texture of the custom-made fabric of his jacket under
her hand, so different from the hard muscles where her
fingers splayed against his chest. She gazed up into his eyes.

The moonlight played on his handsome, chiseled features, reminding her of how much she missed him. Her nipples tightened. Thoughts of him dancing with Lady Luisa invaded her mind. Then—far worse—an image of him making love with Lady Luisa. His arm tightened around her waist when she missed a step.

How would she go on once he married Luisa? Tears stung her eyes. His engagement was imminent. He'd told her the plan was for an August wedding. *Steven is my strength.*

She melted into Massimo's powerful arms, her cheek against his shoulder while they swayed to the music. The rich sound as the bow drew across the strings of violin mixed with the sound of waves lapping at the shore. Moonlight silvered the water. She struggled to hold back the tears that threatened to spill down her cheeks. The lump in her throat choked her. Everything had worked against her. She fought the pain that lodged itself under her breasts. Once the music ended, she stayed in his embrace, her heart fluttering.

"Let's walk along the beach." He sounded gruff.

"Yes." Her voice was barely a whisper. She nodded. *Is he as affected as I am?*

With a flick of his hand, the six guards stationed along the water's edge were dismissed. They receded into the stillness of the night. Stars twinkled in the vastness of the midnight-blue sky, and the full moon cast a silver path from the water along the sandy beach where they strolled. Taking in a breath of the fresh sea air, she said, "I love the water… the sound of the waves is so relaxing."

"It is at that. I enjoy the time I spend here." His thumb rubbed along her wrist as they continued along the beach. "We should go back," he said.

"Okay." She didn't recognize her own voice as it whispered out of her. The scent of his cologne teased her senses, and she had to turn away from him.

The nine-hundred-year-old stone castle stood majestically bathed in moonlight, its round turrets looming tall. Lights from inside the castle spilled out and cast a soft glow through the pointed stained-glass windows.

"I studied medieval design, both Romanesque and Gothic, as an undergraduate. I spent a semester traveling to a few famous castles. Windsor Castle in England, naturally, is the most famous. Then, in Spain… and Italy has the most, all beautiful and special in their own ways."

"Is that so? You studied architecture before engineering."

"No, it was all part of the civic engineering curriculum. I always wanted to be a structural engineer."

"Well then, I will have to show you one of my favorite places in the castle. This is small by some standards, only 110 rooms with just a few outer houses for the staff and the stables. Come," he said.

They walked around the castle, along the base of a high outer wall to a secluded path lined by low-to-the-ground landscape lights. Massimo pushed on a narrow wooden door, and it creaked open. He entwined his fingers with hers, and they stepped into the low-lit entry. A whiff of damp earth drifted through the crude stone hallway. Out of the shadows, two uniformed guards hurried forward, their automatic rifles at the ready. "At ease, men," Massimo said.

The guards stopped short and bowed their heads. "Your Majesty," they said in unison. Then one added, "Our apologies."

"For doing your job? Good work." The overhead lights brightened, and they continued walking down the corridor.

"Where are we going?" Emma whispered. The air was musty, no longer the fresh scent of the sea.

"You'll see," Massimo said, and they walked down another narrow corridor. The walls here were bare and uneven stone. He led her past a stone stairway and stopped.

"The ingenuity of the medieval man, to include a modern elevator." She covered a giggle. He depressed the button on the side panel, and the single aluminum door silently slid open. "My ancestors were forward thinkers," he said, playing along.

The elevator wasn't as fancy or wide as the ones in the main part of the castle. Massimo depressed the button labeled six on the panel. The door closed. The upward motion went on for a few moments. When the door slid open, they faced outside. Emma gasped. Turning to him, she said, "The battlements." They stepped out onto the three-foot-wide wall walk.

"One of my favorite parts of the castle."

"You know, one of the first battlements was built in Egypt, and even the Great Wall of China has them. Pompeii —" Emma looked at the stone floor before he lifted her chin with his finger. She gazed into his blue eyes that reminded her of a cloudless summer day. "I'm sorry; I'm going on and on." Her heart raced. *Kiss me.*

He dropped his hand. "Your excitement is refreshing," he said and stepped away, moving closer to the edge.

She peeked through one of the gaps in the battlements. "You can appreciate the thickness of the walls from here." A cool breeze from the sea swept upward, and she shivered.

Massimo shrugged out of his jacket and placed it around her shoulders. His body heat and his heady scent enveloped her. Holding the jacket closed, she gazed up at the stars. He stood a breath away from her. "I imagine the sky is almost as dark as it was before the castle was built."

Emma peered over the wall and saw the lights of a building. "Are those buildings the stables?"

"Yes. Tomorrow, Steven can stay with his nanny, and we'll go for a ride."

She jumped at the chance to spend more time with him. "I

would like that." *What is wrong with me? This feels like a date, and I just agreed to go riding with him. I have to be stronger than this. The words come out of my mouth, but I don't mean them. I want him to take me in his arms, take me to his bed. I want to forget... that we can't ever be a couple.*

Massimo laced his long fingers with hers and tugged her along, leading her back the way they came. "I'll take you to your room."

"I'm glad you know your way—since I'm lost."

"One wrong turn can lead to the dungeon." He grinned.

"The dungeon?" she said.

"Red, I would never confine you, and we haven't used a dungeon in over a century." He pushed open a door, and Emma breathed a sigh of relief when she saw the marble floor and crystal chandeliers.

The pale-yellow glow was inviting as they walked past several footmen standing at attention. Back on familiar ground, they rode the elevator up to the third floor.

Earlier, for a brief time, she'd forgotten he was the King of Malagra, steeped in traditions and bound by his oath to marry someone else. He'd been Maxy. Emma opened the door to her room and stepped in.

"Emma…" His husky erotic murmur filled her with long-ing. She turned and he pulled her close into his powerful arms. His cologne mixed with virile man—she wanted to experience all the things he could make her feel. She needed the man, not the title. She didn't care that he was a king and a powerful ruler. To her, he was Maxy, the man she'd met in Rome, the man who'd swept her off her feet, the father of her child. She laid her head on his shoulder. His powerful arms tightened around her. "Emma, I need you," he growled.

"I want you so much. The way we were in Rome," she whispered.

He framed her face between his big hands, a spark

ignited, burning deep in his blue eyes. He bent down, and his lips touched hers. The tip of his tongue ran along the seam of her lips. She parted them, welcoming his exploration of her mouth.

She rose on her toes to better fit against him and tangled her fingers in his thick, black hair, holding Massimo to her. Emma melted into his rock-hard body. She breathed in his spicy scent, and the kiss intensified. Rocking her hips against his hard body, she tasted the sexy flavor of his tongue. Her nipples tightened.

The outline of his desire pressed against her belly as heat engulfed her. His hands slipped from her waist to cup her buttocks, dragging her into him.

She whispered, "I need you, Maxy."

One hand moved from her butt and along the back of her leg. He slipped his hand under the hem of her silky slip dress. Fire danced through her when his palm touched her naked leg, sliding the silver fabric up to her waist. She wiggled against him, his knee between her legs as he held her against the wall. Her fingers fumbled at the buttons of his silk shirt. He separated the fabric for her, taking her hands and laying them on his naked chest.

"Better," he said and bent to kiss her. He dragged her into him, his big hands gliding up her torso to her back. He growled, "Where is the damn zipper?"

She rolled her hips against him, her hands spread over his chest, her fingers in his fine chest hair. His heart thudded under her palm.

Massimo groaned, "There is no help for this." He tugged. The sound of fabric tearing registered in her desire-filled mind.

"I'll buy you a new dress," he murmured against her neck before nipping her flesh.

"You bought me this one," she said.

She felt his smile before he lifted his dark head. She couldn't take her eyes away from him as his smile spread, lighting up the room. Massimo tore the remainder of the lustrous dress from her excited body. He slipped his hands under her knees, and she wrapped her legs around his waist. Her head rolled against the wall. His lips started at her neck and moved down to her cleavage.

Her fingers stroked through his thick hair. "Please, Maxy."

Massimo cradled her buttocks in his hands and walked to her bed. Laying her on the cool sheets, he straddled her. His handsome face above her was intense with desire. A lock of black hair fell over his brow. They didn't talk, the time for talking was long gone. Emma knew what this meant. Massimo stripped her of the new lacy silver bra and panties. She pushed his silk shirt off his shoulders. He rose from the bed long enough to unzip his fly and take off his pants, along with the remainder of his clothes. "How long do we have before Steven wakes up?"

She smiled up at him, her heartbeat elevated and wisps of her breath carried her words, "I asked his nanny to take care of him for the night."

The blue of his eyes flared. "You did? I'm glad we're on the same page." He looked like a Roman statue, standing next to the bed, all sculpted muscle upon bulging muscle. His erection left nothing to her imagination. He wanted her, and her core throbbed in response. Her lower abdomen sizzled with heat as she knelt on the edge of the bed, looping her arms around his powerful neck. He cupped an eager breast, exciting the nipple with his thumb and finger before he lowered his head. She couldn't contain the moan of pleasure when the heat of his mouth engulfed her nipple. He sucked the turgid point deep into his mouth. His tongue teased her, and liquid fire spread into her pelvis.

The tips of her fingers skimmed down his torso over

bunched muscles, hard as rocks. "Massimo, please, I don't want to wait anymore."

"We'll save slow for next time." He walked over to his pants, picked them up from the floor, and removed a handful of condoms from his pocket. She couldn't hide the smile that spread across her face. The merry laugh that escaped her when he gazed into her eyes. He tipped his head and lifted a broad shoulder. "I'm prepared."

"I see, very prepared, but actually... I didn't... say anything before. I'm using birth control. Sooo... you really don't need those if you—"

His smile spread. His pants dropped to the Persian rug with a muted thud, followed by a clatter from the foil-wrapped condoms. Emma lay back against the pillows and stretched her arms out to him. "Hurry Maxy, hurry."

"My flesh deep in you. Your tight heat surrounding me." He sauntered to the bed. Her breath caught in her lungs, his broad shoulders and defined pecs filled her vision. Her gaze traveled down his six pack and lower.

He knelt. "Yes. That is my wildest dream of you and me, Red." His hands stroked her, before he took her into his arms and rolled over on the bed. Emma gasped before she smiled, gazing into his sapphire eyes. "Oh, you want me—"

"On top to start."

The next several hours they spent in bed would never leave her mind. He was the Maxy from Rome, laughing and joking with her. No longer the powerful duty-bound King of Malagra, the man who hid all of his emotions. Was she deluding herself, thinking that this could work even though Massimo was tender as always with his care of her? Making sure she reached her peaks of pleasure before he anchored her hips in his enormous hands, surging deep into her core, filling her.

They slept, then in the hour before dawn, he brushed a

kiss on her brow and said, "It's best that I go to my room. After breakfast, we can go to the stables."

"Yes, I would like that." Emma held him to her for one more kiss.

"I will see you in a few brief hours."

"Okay, Maxy."

CHAPTER 13

$\mathcal{E}$xactly as planned the following morning, Massimo strolled into the nursery. He wore a white shirt open at the collar, cuffs turned up, and a gold Rolex encircled his left wrist. His signet ring shone on his left pinky. Fawn-colored riding pants clung to his thighs, and black leather boots completed his outfit.

"Hello," he said. Steven stretched out his chubby arms, wanting to be picked up. "The nanny can take care of Steven while we go for a ride."

Her mouth dried when she glanced at his narrow waist and further down, remembering— "I … Massimo, last night—"

"Was beautiful. We're meant for each other—"

"Don't say that."

Massimo grinned at her before he nodded. "Yes, Red. I've known it from the beginning." He picked Steven up from his crib. Cradling him in his arms, he said, "Are you ready to eat?" The baby shrieked with excitement, putting his tiny fist into his mouth. He chuckled. "You know Mommy is preparing your bottle."

Warmth radiated through her at his word—Mommy. She hurried to make Steven's bottle, and Massimo followed her to the chair.

"I will feed him."

Emma couldn't answer; her throat clogged with tears. She nodded, and Massimo sat in the blue velvet armchair. She handed him Steven's bottle before she placed a bib around the baby's neck. She sat on the matching ottoman and watched her son being fed by his father. Too many emotions clamored in her: joy, elation, and finally, an inkling of something she dared not name. Hope.

Once Steven was down for his nap, Emma rang for the nanny, then she hurried to dress in the riding outfit Massimo had given her.

"Do you ride often?" she asked.

"I do early in the mornings before I begin my official duties. In Santino, the palace's stable is surrounded by a lush and beautiful park, so I take full advantage of that."

"Don't expect a seasoned equestrian in me."

He curled his fingers around her waist, and his sapphire-blue eyes trimmed with long, thick lashes held her gaze. "I remember last night…at one point, you rode me well."

Heat shot into her cheeks, and she dipped her head, turning away from him. They walked down to the stables where his groom had saddled Massimo's horse, a solid black stallion named Forza and for her, a chestnut mare with white socks named Bella.

"This is different from a park. Riding through the morning surf can be invigorating."

"I had some lessons as a child and used to ride through Central Park. As I said before, I haven't ridden in a long time." His rumble of laughter brought a smile to her lips. They trotted out of the stable yard and down to a well-packed dirt path. Tufts of sea grass were scattered along the trail to the beach. The white sandy shore of the castle grounds stretched out before them, with the blue sky and the turquoise Mediterranean meeting on the distant horizon. Motorboats crisscrossed in the distance and closer to shore, one motorboat rode nearby.

She glanced at the man beside her. In the stable, he'd rolled his shirt sleeves up to his elbows, and now, his white shirt clung to him, and his riding pants were molded to his body—man and beast were one. Bella was a gentle mare, and Emma relaxed into the saddle. The surf, with its white foam edges and the smell of the salty sea, was a memory she would tuck away to keep when she was back home.

Massimo commanded his stallion. "No, Forza, we won't be galloping today." The horse snorted before he shook his black mane and picked up his front hooves. Bella shied away, and Emma's heart skipped a beat as Massimo brought Forza under control. His thigh muscles shifted as he used his knees to let the horse know who was in charge of the ride. He held the reins, and Emma swallowed, watching the muscles in Massimo's forearms elongate and flex under his olive skin. Forza shook his shiny black mane once more before settling into an easy trot. Massimo slowed his horse down, and they meandered along the water's edge.

They trotted to a secluded patch of grass. As Massimo jumped off his horse, the muscles in his body rippled, and an errant lock of his black hair fell over his brow. His blue eyes gleamed in the late-morning sunlight. Lifting his arms, his hands went around her waist, and he helped her off her horse. "This would be a nice place for a picnic with Steven," she said.

His arm came around her shoulders as they walked, then he glanced around. "Would you like that?"

"A blanket on the grass. Maybe some wine and cheese for us. I would like that very much."

"I'll call Nicolo and have him arrange it for three o'clock."

"Hmmm, why don't I talk with your chef? Francesco can help me plan something for us. Steven is easy, just formula."

He tugged her into his arms, kissing her brow. "Ah Red, that does sound good. We should head back to the stables. I don't want you to overexert your lovely backside." He wiggled his brows. "I want to play later."

She was just as cheeky. "Have I told you I love the way you play?

They were going to have dinner on the terrace. Emma chose a sleeveless cream-colored mini dress from the clothes Massimo had given her. She slicked on pale-coral lipstick and hurried to brush her hair into soft waves that cascaded down around her shoulders. Emma rushed out to the terrace where Massimo stood, gazing at the water. He wore a dark suit. When she walked out into the warmth of the Mediterranean evening, he turned to her, a smile on his sculpted lips. "I can see the color of your hair in the sunset."

"Maxy, it's you who takes my breath away."

He handed her a glass of wine. She accepted it, and they touched glasses before she took a sip. They peered out over the water at the setting sun in silence. She leaned her head on his shoulder, and he slipped his arm around her waist.

"I have dinner set up on my terrace," he said. Slipping her hand into his, they walked along the low stone wall. Potted plants in groups of three lined the way around the corner to where his terrace connected with hers. Tall candelabras stood on the stone floor. As dusk darkened the sky to evening, a single star flickered. The candles cast a romantic light over the terrace. Soothing violin music filled the air.

Francesco, along with several waiters, stood ready to serve them. A pale-blue cloth covered the intimate table that was set with his finest monogrammed china. Crystal flutes caught the candlelight and reflected off the sterling silver flatware. A vase of pink roses had been placed in the middle of the table. The roses always reminded her of Rome and how he'd run the velvet petals around her breasts before going down her torso and over her abdomen. Massimo held her chair out for her. She sat on the deep-blue velvet high-back dining chair. He moved to sit opposite her, and a footman came forward, holding Massimo's chair for him. Once seated, he nodded, and Francesco came over.

"Your Majesty, Ms. Harris, tonight, I have prepared burrata, a delicate mozzarella and fresh marinated tomatoes, a minestrone, a seabass with a seafood sauce, and for dessert, a tiramisu."

"Splendid, you may begin," Massimo said, and the first course was placed before them. Their crystal glasses were filled with wine.

"I enjoyed today very much."

"As did I. We will have to incorporate a morning ride every day," he said as they finished eating. "Are you ready for a stroll in the gardens?"

"Yes." Emma turned to the chef. "Thank you, Francesco. The meal was superb as always." She smiled at the way he blushed over her praise.

Massimo led her further around his terrace to a sitting area where a footman waited with two snifters of brandy. Once he'd served them, the man bowed to Massimo and left the terrace.

Emma stood near the balcony, sipping the brandy. "The first time I had an after-dinner brandy was with you in Rome."

"I remember the time I poured some on you, then indulged in drinking it from your sexy body."

A smile spread across her lips, her eyes closed, and she sighed. "Yes, I do remember that, but right now, all of this rich food has made me sleepy."

"Come sleep in my arms, then… I can wake you with kisses."

"Oh, that sounds heavenly. Shall we go back to my room?" She leaned into his hard body.

"No, it's too far. We're here." He held her hand and led her from the terrace into his suite. Nothing except perhaps his bedroom at the palace prepared her for his bed here at the castle by the sea. The room was all navy blue and gold with hints of cream. His bed was on a dais and above that, a gold crown and from the crown, yards and yards of sheer gold fabric draped over the side. The headboard was engraved with his monogram. The bed had been turned down for the night.

Massimo scooped her into his arms and spun around with her. She looped her arms tighter around his neck and threw her head back, laughing with him. "Oh, now, I'm no longer sleepy. I want you right here, right now."

His brow shot up. "Standing in the middle of the room?"

"Yes, just your strong, masculine body holding me."

His kryptonite smile took her breath away as he stood her on the blue-and-gold Persian carpet. Her feet sank into the plushness, and she unzipped the side zipper on her mini dress. He tugged her into his arms, and his lips moved over hers in a tender kiss before she slipped her tongue into his mouth. At that, he lifted her against him, sucking on her tongue, then he steadied her on her feet once more to lift her dress over her head. Massimo bent to suck her nipple through the sheer fabric of her bra before he unclasped it. "You're beautiful."

Emma couldn't wait to see him naked. She pushed his jacket off his broad shoulders while he toed off his shoes. She ran her open palms up over the silk fabric of his shirt before reaching for the buttons.

"Let me, Red." Massimo grabbed the placard in both

hands and separated the white silk fabric. She giggled as some of his shirt buttons flew in every direction to silently land on the Persian carpet. He unfastened his waistband. Emma stepped closer into his arms. Her hand slipped over the fabric that covered his erection. "No talking, Maxy, only this in me, now," she said, moving her hand up and down over the bulge before giving him a playful squeeze.

His erotic laugh sizzled up her spine as he dropped to his knees. Massimo kissed her belly, then lower along her abdomen, dragging the scrap of lace down her legs. He nuzzled her, and Emma cupped his head, smoothing his thick, black hair from his brow.

"Maxy, yes, yes."

Massimo held her butt cheeks, massaging her. He lifted his head. "How does that feel? Any soreness from this morning's ride?"

"No. Everything feels really good." His smile melted her as he tugged her closer. Her breath caught as he spread her for his mouth. She couldn't hold back the moan when his tongue touched her sensitive skin.

Massimo sucked, and she rose on her toes, fitting herself better to his mouth. Her fingers tangled in his black hair.

Heat spread through her core as the muscles in her abdomen tightened. His tongue probed before he stroked her most sensitive skin, lapping at the bundle of nerves. Emma was on fire. Her head fell forward, her eyes closed, and all she needed was Massimo to soothe the burning inferno he'd started. His masterful tongue stroked her again and again before he sucked her clit. She needed him to do that again.

"Oh Maxy, yes, yes, ahh… Oh… So… Good." She was grateful his big hands held her and kept his mouth on her until the last shudder left her body.

Only then did he stand. "I love the sounds you make," he

said, dropping his pants. He lifted Emma. "I need to feel you come again, this time with your heat surrounding me."

Emma wrapped her arms around his neck as her legs came around his waist. "I can't wait," she said, cupping his cheeks and pressing her lips on his. She loved how he took control of the kiss, sliding his tongue in to mesh and mate with hers. Her taste mingled with his to make her wild. She rubbed her breasts, and the sensitized nipples into the mat of Massimo's silky black chest hair. A groan escaped her. He held her in place before he thrust and entered her in one smooth motion. "You feel really, really good."

He growled, "Then let's see how you feel when I put the rest of me in you." Holding her buttocks, he thrust again while lowering her on his long steel-hard shaft.

"Oh, yes," Emma cried out, feeling weightless in his arms. All it took was a handful of strokes, and she couldn't help herself. Her muscles tightened before releasing as waves of ecstasy washed over her, and he drove her to a second orgasm. She held onto his shoulders as her head fell back. Massimo kissed her neck, licking her heated skin. "Oh God, I love this so much," she moaned.

"Shall I make you come again?"

"Yes, more. I'm greedy for you."

He lowered her onto him as he thrust up, filling her completely. Then he did the most amazing thing. He walked over to the nearest wall and leaned her against it. "Hold on, Red." He pulled almost completely out, and Emma tried to hold him in her, squirming and moving her hips. "Look at me," he said.

She lifted her gaze to his, then he thrust into her, grinding and pistoning in and out again and again. "Maxy... I'm going... to... come." She locked her ankles around his narrow hips. Holding on to him. Thankful for the wall at her back for support.

"I know, Red. I can feel you're wet and oh so tight heat surrounding me, clenching me." He groaned, digging his fingers into her ass. She felt the eruption of his orgasm deep in her core, taking everything he offered. Every muscle on his hard body bulged. Holding her on him as he shouted her name, and she kissed the crook of his neck and along one shoulder. Only then did she realize that both their bodies were covered in a fine mist from their sexual exertion.

Massimo smiled in the semi-dark room. "Emma, my redheaded beauty, this image of us will forever be seared on my brain…to my dying day." He caressed her lips with a soft kiss.

"I'm not sure I can walk," she sighed before her legs slipped down his flanks.

He grinned, lifting a brow at her. Massimo bent, and his arm went under her knees to lift her. "It will be my pleasure to carry you to my bed."

Massimo held Emma in his arms. She'd fallen asleep after that last orgasm. Her red locks were streaming over his forearm, and her hair brushed across his bare chest, stirring him. She sighed in her sleep. "Maxy… my love."

His brow furrowed and he gazed down at her. *Did I hear right?* His heart thumped wildly in his chest. Her soft breath against his neck Massimo held her tighter to him and strolled from his room.

Emma murmured, "Where are you taking me?"

He breathed in her jasmine scent. "Back to your bedroom." He walked silently into her room and laid Emma down before he climbed in and molded himself around her soft, luscious curves. He pulled the satin cover over them. She snuggled more comfortably into him before kissing his neck. "Stay with me," she said with a sigh.

Always. "I'm not going anywhere." *Ever.* Massimo kissed her brow and held her through the night, guarding her sleep while thoughts of Emma kept him awake. The first streaks of dawn were lighting the sky when Emma stirred in his arms.

"Mmm, I thought this was a dream. You did spend the night with me." Emma stretched her arms over her head, then she rolled into him before she brushed her soft, sleep warm lips over his mouth.

Massimo caressed her curvy body, cupping a breast. "This is so much better," he said against her neck.

"What time is it?"

"I think we have a little while for more loving before Steven wakes up."

She whispered in her soft sexy voice, "How did you know what I was thinking?" She lifted her leg to lie across his and rolled on top of him. Her shapely legs tangled with his, and she planted kisses along his jaw, down his neck, and across his chest.

Stroking her hair, his fingers glided through the long heavy mass of copper curls.

Massimo sat up with her draped over him. "Because you and I have the same thoughts." Taking her lips once more while his hands found her breasts, rubbing the nipples between his thumbs and forefingers, he felt them harden. Her green eyes filled with desire.

Emma reached between them as her fingers drifted over his abdomen before taking his erection, rubbing her thumb over the head. She kissed his shoulder and into the crook of his neck while her hand wrapped around him as her thumb slid over and around the head of his erection.

He groaned, and Emma let out a sexy, seductive laugh before she nipped his earlobe.

She whispered, "Why don't we go into the shower–"

"Shower sex? Red, you have the best ideas." He stood and lifted her over his shoulder.

As he headed for the ensuite, Emma smacked his butt.

Her musical laughter floated around them. He stood her on her feet, and she reached into the huge glass-enclosed shower to turn on the sprays.

She tugged him to her, wrapping her arms around his neck as she walked backwards, dragging him under the gentle spray. "This may sound crazy... I like the feel of your morning stubble."

"Where?" He kissed her soft lips and down the satin smoothness of her neck.

She stood before him, petite and perfect. The green of her eyes intensified, looking like two polished emeralds, and her hands reached to caress his shoulders.

"Here?" He cupped a breast before he bent his head to run his chin along a pointed nipple.

"Oh, yes, I like that." She dug her fingers into his hair.

"And the other?" He pulled her against him, feasting on her other breast.

"Most definitely," she sighed, pressing her lethal body into him.

He dropped to his knees. "What about this?" He ran his morning stubbled chin along her soft belly. "And lower... over here?"

"Yes... Maxy... right... there."

CHAPTER 14

Freshly showered, Massimo left Emma and returned to his own room. Not needing his valet this morning, he went into his ensuite to shave and dress for the day, reliving the pleasant hour he and Emma had just spent together. And last night? When Emma had sighed, *my love*, in her sleep, his heart wrenched and in that instant, he'd known what he wanted. His desire for Emma won the battle. Heart over duty. He would find a way to have her. He was bound by his oath to marry someone with a royal bloodline, and that was Luisa, not Emma.

Massimo, casual in jeans and a polo shirt, went to his study and called his solicitor. He told him what he wanted—to legitimize Steven's birth and make him his heir. His attorney would get on it immediately and draw up the papers. Once he ended the call with his personal attorney, he asked Nicolo to come to his study. Nicolo was more than his chief aide. They had served in the military together and had always been close friends. When he arrived, he said, "Good morning Your Majesty," closing the door behind him.

"Yes, it is a wonderful morning. You know that baby boy is my son."

"Yes, sir. Do you wish to order a discreet paternity test?"

Massimo frowned at his aide. "No. Not at all. That may become necessary at some point, although my acknowledgement is more than enough. What I want is to change the damn law that prevents me from marrying Emma Harris."

"Your Majesty…"

"Don't look so surprised. We are steeped in traditions and ceremonies, but that law is very oppressive to me. As absolute monarch, it is my right to change any laws that are outdated for the good of the citizens of Malagra. That law restricts my happiness, and I too am a citizen of this country. I am taking the first steps to abolish that provision in the Succession to the Crown Act. I want this done well before the opening of Parliament. There will be no vote. It will be done because I deem it so.

I want you to schedule a meeting with the prime minister. Don't make it sound like a summons even though it is. I want to see him today. Earlier, I spoke with my attorney, and he is preparing a decree naming Steven Max Harris my heir. I have instructed him to add a codicil to my will leaving one of my estates along with the land and sufficient funds to Emma as the mother of the future king. I will name my mother Queen Gabriella regent should anything happen to me before…"

"Sir!"

"Calm yourself, Nicolo. I must prepare for all circumstances but believe me, I plan on living a very long life. Only you and my attorney know my intentions with Steven. The prime minister just needs to know that I intend to change the Succession to The Crown Act."

"I understand, Your Majesty."

Later that day, Massimo sat on a chaise lounge on the terrace, his long legs stretched out before him. Steven was on his lap, playing a new game he'd just invented. Emma had brought out her laptop to check her email—she'd mentioned that she wanted to see how the hospital was progressing. "What exactly does a king do?"

At that moment, Massimo was bouncing Steven on his knees before letting him slide down his legs onto his lap. Steven giggled, then let out a big belly laugh in anticipation of the next time he got to slide down.

Massimo looked at her, sitting on the terrace, her laptop on the table, and a cup of coffee beside it. Her hair was loose and flowing down around her shoulders. "Do you mean besides this… and what we did to make him?"

"Don't—"

"The monarchy is steeped in traditions, and we certainly do love our ceremonies." He'd made light of the subject until he saw how serious Emma had become. "I have quite a busy schedule filled with state events. I am the patron of many organizations and charities. Next month, I have a ground-breaking ceremony scheduled for the new hospital."

"Really?"

"Yes, and Gino has already been in contact with your company. We are planning for two more hospitals to be built after this one."

"I didn't know."

"Yes, it is much more than ribbon cutting, you know. The first of June is the opening of Parliament. I have begun working on my speech. The entire royal family is in atten-dance. The women dress in gowns and wear their best tiaras, while the men wear their uniforms. We have a procession from the palace to Parliament. I wear my uniform and my crown."

Her eyes rounded.

"Why so surprised?" he asked.

"I'm sorry. I recall a photo of you with your crown, robe, and scepter." Emma typed on her keyboard. "Here, look." She turned her laptop toward him.

"Yes, one of my official portraits from my coronation. A robe, yes, but no scepter for the opening of Parliament."

"Then what happens?"

"After that, from the throne I give a speech and lay out my plans for Malagra in the upcoming year. With the help of the prime minister and my ministers, we work to better the lives of the people of Malagra."

"I read that this is an absolute monarchy and that you have two brothers and a sister. Do they help?"

"Also nieces, nephews, and cousins, uncles and aunts. And yes, once they turn eighteen, they begin their Royal duties. At that time, they choose a favorite charity and I give them permission to become patron of it."

"That's interesting— you have to agree to their choices."

"More than agree, Emma. I give them *my* permission."

Emma folded her hands in her lap before she lifted her gaze to him. "I guess I always knew you had unchecked power." She leaned in. "But what do you really do? You don't have commitments every day."

"I have what you refer to as commitments, and I don't have a typical nine-to-five schedule. I'll be hosting my cousin King Filippo and his wife, Queen Sarina of San Destino. There will be a state dinner and other functions scheduled for next month. In May, I go on a three-day state visit to Spain."

"You are very busy."

"Yes, and there are some things that I look forward to more than others. In two weeks, on Wednesday, is King's Day."

"King's Day," she echoed. "What's that?"

"My birthday. The country celebrates the day I was born."

"Really. You mean the entire country? Do they sing happy birthday?"

"Yes, and there is a parade. In the evening, there is a ball, fireworks, and a cake baked by the palace pastry chef. It is a great honor to be king. The week before, my mother organizes a private celebration, just the family. Dinner and cake."

"Yes and a daunting schedule I would imagine."

"No, schedules are our friend, as one of my nannies loved to say. All this is in service to my country."

"I hadn't realized how packed your days are."

"It's not all work. There are some fun times too. This time with you and Steven is the best."

"Yes, this is nice." Emma closed her laptop. "Shouldn't we discuss arrangements before Steven and I go home?"

"No, not yet. I have begun," Massimo cut himself off, not prepared to tell her his intentions. "We can discuss all of that later. For now, let's have lunch."

He called for the nanny to take Steven.

"I think you're trying to postpone the inevitable," Emma said.

"Very astute, Ms. Harris. I would rather avoid an argument with you."

"Oh, is that it? You know for certain that there will be a disagreement?"

"Yes. So, I prefer to eat lunch without a side of indigestion."

She giggled. "I grant you a reprieve, Your Majesty."

He lifted a dark brow at her. She was too cheeky, and he loved their banter. "What else will you grant me?"

"Oh, I don't know… let me think."

He dragged her into him, then sat with her on his lap. "Kiss me."

"Yes, Maxy." She held his cheeks between her hands and bent her head to him. The kiss began slowly with feather light brushes of her lips over his. He slid his hand under her blouse, delaying lunch for an hour while they enjoyed each other.

CHAPTER 15

It was the middle of their second week, and time was ticking away, with less than a handful of days remaining before she and Steven would return to Brooklyn. Massimo lay in Emma's bed, holding her in his arms. They were both awake and watching as the sun rose, turning the sky to streaks of pink and orange. "I'll get dressed. We can give Steven his bath, then we can have breakfast and spend a leisurely morning here on the terrace."

"Mmm, that sounds divine," she said.

Massimo rose from the bed, and Emma held her breath. She couldn't get enough of looking at his naked body. Right now, his sculpted backside, with his perfect butt, always stopped her. How was he so flawless and beautiful? He turned to her as he stepped into his pants, not bothering to fully raise his fly. His pants rode low on his narrow hips. "Stop staring so, or I won't go. The nanny can take care of our son."

Emma rose on her elbow. "You accuse me of Maxy staring?" She giggled before she covered her eyes. "Hurry, go," she said. "Before I take you up on your offer."

He returned a short time later in jeans and a polo shirt. Steven was bathed and fed. Now, he played in his crib. Massimo suggested having coffee on the terrace while they listened to Steven over the baby monitor. He was making sounds as if he were trying to talk, then giggling. "He's entertaining himself," Massimo said.

"I thought he was going to crawl, but it's too early. He just rolled over the other day."

Massimo smiled at her. "Don't you have that information tucked away in one of your many baby books? I saw your extensive collection of childcare literature at your home. I'll call in the royal pediatrician, and you can talk with her. She's cared for my nieces and nephews."

"No, I did a quick search on the internet, and it's too soon."

Steven shrieked again before he gurgled and laughed, playing some more, then he shrieked again.

"I'll get him," Massimo said, laughing.

"He probably needs a clean diaper," she said.

"That's okay. Why don't you pour us another cup of coffee? I'll take care of our son."

Emma hurried and changed into a green short-sleeved cotton sundress. She poured the coffee, then waited for Massimo. He returned, carrying Steven over to her. Massimo flashed her a smile, the kind that always made her knees weak. "He has a clean diaper and now, he wants to play."

"Oh really. Come to Mama, my handsome boy." She held her hands out, and Steven tipped in her direction.

Massimo sat on the double chaise lounge next to Emma. "Shall we relax by the pool or go to the beach?"

"The beach, please. Can we have lunch there?"

"I like that idea. A casual meal on the beach."

Nicolo requested permission to enter. "Your Majesty,

Miss Harris, excuse the interruption. A matter has arisen that requires your attention."

He frowned. "What is it that can't wait?"

Nicolo looked at Emma, then back to Massimo.

"You can speak in front of Miss Harris."

"Your Majesty… your mother has arrived."

Emma gasped. "Oh no."

The world was intruding on their privacy, reminding her once again that this was a sham. She was going back to her life in New York, and he would marry Lady Luisa. They played at being a family, but she'd always known this was fake and could never be more. The foundation was built on a fantasy and had begun to crack. *What did I expect? After I so easily fell into his bed? He never lied to me, and there isn't anything he can do. We're both trapped.*

Massimo sat forward on the lounge. "Keep her in the main drawing room until I come down."

Nicolo bowed his head. "Yes, Your Majesty," he said and left the terrace.

Massimo grinned. "Well, it's about time Steven met his grandmother." He ruffled Steven's black hair.

Emma tried to keep the anger from her voice. "Is that all you can say?"

He glanced at her, a frown creasing his brow. "At the moment, yes. I'll go change out of these jeans, then talk to her. Perhaps I can convince my mother to return to Santino. Although I do believe I know why she's here. I did tell you that my birthday is next week, and we usually have the family dinner the week before."

Steven cried out, and Emma held him to her. "I feel over-whelmed," she said, continuing to rub his back. "He needs his bottle, then I'm putting him down for a nap. Massimo, I will stay in my room until your mother leaves."

He bent and kissed her brow. "I understand how you're

feeling, but this is a good thing, perhaps sooner than I cared for. You'll see that all of this will work out. I haven't mentioned much to you, Red, but I have been quite busy working on a plan that will be best for you and me. We will talk about our future and Steven's."

She couldn't keep the anger from coming through in her voice. "Really, a plan. Wow, tell me more. Is it something similar to what your ancestor did keeping—"

"That is uncalled for. You know the true story now," he cut through her words. "I will return after I dress and before I talk with my mother."

She scowled at him. Massimo let out a slow breath before he wrapped his arms around her and Steven. He leaned in and placed a kiss on her brow and the tip of her nose.

He left to go to his room. Emma was mortified. Her bubble had really burst. How could she so easily forget that he was going to marry someone else? Holding Steven against her, she hurried from the terrace into her bedroom and through to the nursery. She laid Steven on the changing table. "You are such a good boy. Mommy loves you so much." A tear splashed on the back of her hand, then another and another. She brushed at them with the heel of her palm, more upset with herself than with Massimo.

Massimo came back dressed in a gray three-piece suit, very similar to the first time she'd seen him in Rome. The arms of the expensive material barely hid his biceps and his broad shoulders. A matching vest emphasized his narrow waist. A custom-made white shirt and a tie in the palest blue. He wore his signet ring and looked every bit the powerful king he was.

"What's this?" He crossed the room and tilted her chin.

"Massimo, I want to go home," an anguished sigh escaped her. "Today, it's your mother, but what happens when Luisa arrives? I don't want her to ever find out about Steven." She took in a ragged breath. "Your mother, I guess that's different naturally… I can't stay. I was foolish to think you could bond with Steven, and I could remain off to the side, out of your life. I can't even stay out of your bed." She bowed her head. "Look at what I'm doing! Sleeping with you when you're virtually engaged to someone else." She wiped her eyes. "This is too much for me right now. Please understand. I have to go home *now*."

"Emma, you agreed to two weeks, and we still have some time." She looked at Massimo, her brow furrowed. *He's selfish, then he'll leave me just like Josh— No. Don't do this to yourself.*

"I have no freedom here. I can't just go at will. I am reliant on you, and I don't like that. I'm independent, making my own decisions and right now—I choose to return home. I have become the other woman. Exactly what I never wanted. I blame myself entirely for giving into my weakness for you. And that is what it is—a weakness, a-a madness. I have no willpower where you're concerned."

"No, Emma, it's not a question of willpower. I don't want you to feel that way. The feelings we have surpass that, and there is so much more. I am truly sorry. What we have is special. I should have said something sooner." He ran his fingers through his hair. "The time we were apart, you are all I thought of and all I wanted." He pulled her to him, and she resisted. "I dragged my feet, delaying my engagement because I have wanted no one but you since Rome."

Her head snapped up, and her mouth rounded.

"Yes, believe me. It's always been you. I thought I could do what was necessary for my country, but I haven't been able to. I cannot bring myself to put a ring on her finger." He moved away.

Emma couldn't say a word. His sincerity was clear.

"I will go and talk with my mother. Will you dress our son so that he can meet his grandmother?"

She nodded, too overwhelmed to actually talk. *What is he saying? I can't be strung along. I have to go home.*

Massimo left the room, closing the door behind him.

MASSIMO WALKED across the drawing room. "Mother, this is a surprise." He leaned down and kissed first one cheek, then the other.

"It took me awhile to find out where you were. Your security and staff are very protective of your privacy, Massimo. It's almost time for the family birthday celebration, and I thought that by now you would have proposed to Luisa. When I spoke with her, she said that you haven't returned her calls, and you've cleared your calendar. What is going on?"

"I came here to get away and have some time to myself."

"Massimo, this is not like you, to shirk your duty. You're a great king. You know that it's time to marry and start a family of your own. Your sister has three children, your brother has two, and at this rate, even Alfonso, who is still at university, will be married before you. Malagra needs your heir. I don't understand what has come over you. I thought that by now, everything was settled between you and Luisa. She said you talked of an August wedding. Well, that doesn't leave much time—"

"No more talk of that." He cut the air with his hand. "I know you don't understand, but you will soon." *I already have an heir.*

"I'll call Luisa—"

"No, you will not," he said, his voice harsher than he intended.

"Massimo! I'm your mother—"

"Yes, but I'm the king, and I don't want Luisa here. As a

matter of fact, I am pleased that you did find me. There is someone I want you to meet."

"Should I be worried?"

"No, not at all. Wait here."

"As you wish." She extended her hands to the side and gave a slight bow.

Massimo left his mother in the drawing room and went back to Emma. He found her sitting in a yellow wing chair, her legs tucked under her, by the cold hearth in her room. She was staring at nothing and looked up when he approached.

Her eyes were red rimmed. "Emma, are you crying?"

She bent her head and wouldn't answer him. Finally, she mumbled, "Steven is napping, and I want to pack my bags."

"No."

Emma glared at him before she turned away. He glanced at the bed, still rumpled from their night together. For the first time, Massimo realized that this was what a loving relationship and family were like. Laughing, playing with their child. Beginning and ending the day together. He wanted that, and he would have it with Emma... Emma, his surprise love. Massimo never had that growing up. He couldn't remember a time when his mother and father acted like a family. She rose from the chair and walked past him, keeping her distance.

Massimo followed Emma as she walked into her dressing room. She lifted her suitcase from the floor and placed it on a bench. Opening it, she began packing. "I'm only taking my clothes and what I brought for Steven."

"No." Massimo somehow kept the anger from his voice. "You can't go."

Emma folded a sundress. "In Brooklyn, before I agreed to come here, you promised me you wouldn't stop me when I wanted to leave." She turned to him. "You gave me your word."

"I know, but we still have a few days, and I don't want you to go. Remember, I did mention that I have a plan." *I never want you to leave me, ever. I just need a little more time.*

Emma focused on the suitcase, adding two pairs of jeans. She opened a drawer and grabbed her tops. "You're going to marry someone else. That's your plan, and I can't be here for that. I won't subject myself to anymore humiliation." She dropped her clothes into the case and turned to him. "It's going to hurt me no matter where I am. I can't stay here any longer. I don't have the willpower to resist you."

He wouldn't tell her more at this moment. "Emma, for now, I would like you and Steven to meet my mother. Now get dressed and come with me."

She faced him with her hands on her hips. "Is that an order, Your Majesty?"

THE GOLD FLECKS in his blue eyes sparkled, and a slow smile spread across his sculpted lips, melting her. "No, it's only a request from Maxy."

Her better judgement lost the argument. She looked up into his handsome face, the dimple in his chin, the bow of his perfect lips, just before the smile returned. All she wanted to do was go to bed with him. Stay in that bubble forever. She stood still and watched him remove one of the many day dresses he had bought her from her wardrobe.

He stood next to her. "Shall I help you with this? Act as lady's maid."

She almost burst out laughing. "I've never needed help to get dressed."

"Ahhh very well, Ms. Harris… then later… I will help strip

this off you." His voice sent zaps of pleasure through her body. She couldn't stay mad at him. Each moment was precious and needed to be tucked away for when she would be alone and all she would have were her memories.

She lifted a brow at him, shaking her head. "You think this is settled?"

"Red, I have learned that nothing is ever as it appears with you." He handed her the outfit. "I will wait in the sitting room while you dress."

Emma nodded and chose a matching bra and panties. *I have to be stronger—I can't give in to my body's desires. He doesn't understand how weak I am where he's concerned.* She glanced at herself in the full-length mirror. She liked the dress he'd picked for her to wear to meet his mother. A cream-colored, short-sleeved, above-the-knee-length silk dress. What made it pretty was the splash of embroidered blue flowers going up the side from the hem and continuing across and up to the opposite shoulder. She stepped into a pair of high heels, the exact color of the flower embellishment of the dress—then she met him in the sitting area of her bedroom.

He stood. "Your beauty is breathtaking."

Emma felt heat rise into her cheeks at his compliment. "I had better get Steven ready." She dressed the baby in a blue cashmere romper with a smocked top, and added white socks and white leather shoes to the outfit. Massimo held Steven as they walked to the wide marble staircase. A red carpet ran down the center to the second floor and continued along the hallway. Urns filled with wildflowers stood on carved marble pedestals along the walls.

"I know this is a big step for you, Red, but this will all work out."

"I can't see how, Massimo. You and Lady Luisa—"

There wasn't any more time to talk. They reached the white-and-gilt double doors. Two footmen bowed their heads, then opened the doors. She and Massimo stepped into the formal drawing room. Floor-to-ceiling gold velvet drapes covered the many windows in the large semicircle room. The floor was highly polished cherrywood, with Persian rugs scattered around. The vaulted ceiling was a work of art, with its fresco and crystal chandeliers.

"Mother, I would like you to meet Miss Emma Harris and our son Steven Max Harris."

The woman who greeted her gave a whole new meaning to the word regal. The queen was the picture of elegance and grace, sitting on a green satin brocade sofa. She wore a raspberry-colored suit with a pale-pink silk blouse beneath the jacket. A diamond and ruby broach was pinned on her right shoulder, and she wore the matching earrings. Her ankles were crossed and on her feet were black designer kitten-heel pumps. Her blond shoulder-length hair was styled in the latest blunt cut fashion. Massimo's mother masked her surprise so quickly, Emma couldn't be sure if the queen actually blinked. *Did she hear him?* One hand with a diamond and ruby ring on her ring finger moved on her lap.

"Miss Harris," she said, adding a smile to her berry-colored lips that didn't quite reach her blue eyes.

Emma extended her hand. The queen ignored her, and she wondered if she should curtsy. Instead, Emma simply said, "Your Majesty."

"Massimo, did you say that this baby is your son?" Her voice held her disdain.

"Yes, Mother. I acknowledge him as my son and, more so, he will be my heir."

Emma gasped. "No." Steven's eyes rounded, and his bottom lip thrust out in a pout, ready to cry.

"Massimo," his mother exclaimed. "No. You know that is impossible."

Emma's voice rose. "What are you saying? We never—I told you he's my son, and we're going home."

"No arguing with me," he thundered.

Emma reached over and lifted Steven out of his arms. She patted Steven's back, comforting her son.

The queen stood, stepping over to them. Her eyes narrowed when she turned to Emma. "Miss Harris, how old is your son?"

"Four months," Emma said.

Massimo's mother pursed her lips and tipped her elegant head to one side. "There is a resemblance. He does look like you, Massimo. All of that thick black hair, and his eyes are blue. Although many babies do have blue eyes." The queen turned to Massimo. "Have you begun DNA testing?"

"I will not allow any testing," Emma blurted.

The queen lifted a well-defined eyebrow. "Miss Harris, we cannot take your word for it. We need proof that is above question. Go back to your room. I would like some time with *my* son. Alone."

Massimo moved beside Emma. "No, Mother, we don't need alone time. As a matter of fact, you should return to Santino."

"I came here to prepare for your birthday celebration."

"No, we will have the dinner at your home in Santino, as always."

"As you wish, but I would like to stay for a few days."

Massimo let out a long sigh. "You may stay, but no more talking of tests. He is my son because I know so. We will leave you to settle in your rooms, and, Mother, I will not tolerate any rudeness to Emma."

The queen bowed her head and gestured her acceptance to Massimo.

CHAPTER 16

The red carpet down the center of the long portrait-strewn corridor muffled their footsteps. They were alone—as alone as the king could be—with footmen and his royal guards stationed at intervals, and Emma allowed Massimo to carry Steven as they returned to the third floor hallway and walked toward the nursery.

"Is that the way you talk to your mother?" Emma asked in surprise.

"Sometimes she forgets I'm the king, so I need to remind her."

"Well, that's very interesting—"

"No more of this." Emma heard impatience which deepened the accent in his voice.

Massimo led her into the nursery, where he gave Steven to his nanny.

"Let's go out to your terrace. We will have privacy there," Massimo said, taking her hand and entwining his long fingers with hers. He opened the glass door to her terrace, leading her to the comfortable double lounger to sit on the yellow-and-white striped cushion. Below them, a fountain gurgled, and the morning air was scented with fresh flowers and rose bushes. Along the low wall of the stone terrace were gardenia plants in large antique planters. Emma loved the purple bougainvillea that climbed up the marble columns and spread across the open arches framing the Mediterranean Sea in the distance.

"Your mother—"

He brought her hand to his lips.

"Massimo, it's time for me to go home. I cannot stay any longer. It was a mistake to come here. Steven and I—"

"No, Red, Malagra is your home now. I meant what I said. Steven will be my heir."

Emma pulled her hand out of his grasp. "I can't see how that will work. I have a life in New York that I am not willing to give up. I'm a single mother and must do what is best for my son. You have obligations that I cannot be a part of, and I won't leave my baby here." She stood and gazed at him, reclining on the lounger. The custom suit jacket was unbuttoned, and his vest accented a narrow waist. She admired his long legs stretched out before him and crossed at the ankle. His muscular body always made her think of other things.

"You heard your mother. Although she tried to hide it behind her royal demeanor, I saw her reaction. She doubts that you're Steven's father. The look she gave me held nothing but contempt. What about the rest of your family? What will they think? Your country?"

"Emma, I will address that later. I know he is my son. I will deal with my mother and her attitude—"

She cut the air with her hand. "Massimo, you are about to make an enormous commitment to Luisa. I'm positive there won't be anything in the vows you two exchange about keeping a mistress. Nor would I ever accept that role."

He stood and wrapped her in his arms. "For now, you do not think about August." Keeping her to his side, he slid his phone from his pocket. Touching the screen with his thumb, he said, "Nicolo, have my mother meet me in my office, now." He slipped his phone back into his pocket.

Her hand landed on her chest. "Oh dear, you meant right this minute."

He nodded. "The sooner the better." He dazzled her with a smile. "I will be back later," he whispered and kissed her brow.

Massimo gazed out the window of his study at the manicured gardens and the sea beyond. He'd brought Emma and his son here to this castle to have privacy from the press and his family.

He needed more time with Emma to convince her—

At the knock on his door, he turned, clearing his thoughts.

Nicolo opened the door and stepped to the side. "Come in, Mother."

Massimo strolled over to his mahogany desk and leaned his hip against the edge. His mother entered, going directly to the sofa, and sat. She waited for Nicolo to close the door behind him.

In a voice filled with exasperation, she said, "You cannot make that child your heir." She threw her hands up in the air. "How can you even consider something so outlandish?" She took an audible breath before she continued, "Once you and Luisa marry, you will start a family. Those children will be your heirs, not an illegitimate son of a commoner and an American at that." Her voice held her dissatisfaction.

Massimo tensed. "Let me be perfectly clear. This is not up for debate. I have made my decision." He raised his voice for emphasis, "Steven will be my heir—the sooner you acknowledge that fact, the better it will be for all concerned."

"Massimo, how can you? You would set aside our traditions and the law that has been in place for generations?"

He controlled his anger before he said, "It is an antiquated law. One made by a tyrannical king who was only interested in power and expanding the kingdom for his gain. Malagra is moving forward, and the ruler should not be hindered by whom he wishes to marry."

"Massimo, this is more than that—"

"Tell me, were you and Father—"

"In love?" she cut in.

He nodded.

His mother held her head high, taking a breath. "Your father and I were acquainted at an early age. When he needed to produce an heir, I was able to accept, having a royal bloodline. Massimo, you know that we were content. We, your father and I, did our duty, giving Malagra three sons and a daughter."

"I desire more than to just be content. I will serve my country as I have and always will. I will do what is best for Malagra, but I want happiness and not just to be content. Yes, I want love. I need a woman who loves me for me, the man, someone who looks past my title."

"You can have that with Luisa. She's been vetted and is cultured. The most important fact is that she is royal. Luisa is prepared to take her place beside you. She is what Malagra needs in a queen. Her intelligence and beauty are added bonuses. You will learn to care for one another. She will honor you and your commitment to Malagra. I know you can be happy together."

"I demand and am entitled to more than that. We will meet for dinner this evening. I would like you to give Emma a chance."

"I prefer to dine alone… while she is here."

He tensed. His mother did not understand how much Emma meant to him, but she would. "Very well. You may dine alone. Let me be perfectly clear. Steven is my rightful heir, and you will have to come to terms with my decision. And one more thing… tomorrow, you will return home to Santino."

"Massimo—"

"Enough—it will be as I wish. There will be no further discussion. Go home," he ordered.

He stormed to the door leading to his aide's office and threw it open. "Nicolo," he shouted. "Queen Gabriella will be returning to Santino tomorrow. Make the arrangements."

"Yes, sir." Massimo closed the door and strode back to the center of the room.

His mother stood before him. "You are my son, and I love you," she said, kissing him on both cheeks. Then, she left his office.

It took Massimo a while for the tension to leave his body and calm down before he strode to his room. He changed out of his suit and pulled on a pair of jeans, grabbing a button-down shirt from a hanger, tucking it into his waistband. He chose a more casual wristwatch from his assortment and left his dressing room to find Emma.

Emma's red hair fell in waves around her. Reclining on the chaise in the bedroom with her feet tucked under her, he smiled to himself. *This is her favorite way to sit and read. Or, for that matter, watch television with me.* He loved the way she would rest her head on his shoulder, at times rubbing her hand over his chest. He couldn't ignore his erection as it pressed against his zipper.

Emma closed and placed her book beside her when he entered. "You survived," she said with a cheeky tone in her voice.

"You doubted me?" He grinned. "I am the king, and in the end, what I want is what I get. Only my mother can and does voice her opinion, but she, too, will come around."

Emma sighed slowly, shaking her head from side to side.

"Let's take Steven for a walk in the gardens. Tonight, we can have a quiet dinner. Just the two of us."

"What about your mother?"

"She is staying in her rooms, then leaving in the morning. Don't look so sad. It's best this way. You can call Francesco and have him prepare your favorite meal."

She frowned at him.

"You know… a sandwich. We can watch a movie on the television," he said.

"Then we can talk," her voice was eager and upbeat.

"Not tonight. I am finished with talking. This evening, we are going to relax. I may take my shoes off and put my feet up on the coffee table."

She lifted her brows at that before she smiled at him. Her green eyes flashed her merriment. "Oh my, the king is letting loose."

"Just Maxy." He wiggled his brows at her.

They had a quiet dinner, something more than a sandwich. She surprised him with one of his favorite meals.

"How did you know?"

"I have my ways." Lifting a shoulder, she said, "I asked Francesco." After dinner had been cleared they decided on a murder mystery to watch on the living room TV.

"Tomorrow, we can go for a ride," he said, kissing her brow.

"We haven't settled anything, and I'm not sure if you pretending that nothing has changed with your mother's arrival is wise."

"You will have to trust me on this. I have our best interests uppermost in my thoughts. Actually, to be fair, right now, all I want is to bury myself deep in your welcoming heat."

She bit the corner of her bottom lip. "Mmmm, that sounds wonderful," she whispered and leaned her sexy curves into him.

LATE THE FOLLOWING MORNING, the sun cast its rays over the water, turning the sea into twinkling diamonds. Massimo and Emma were out on horseback, riding through the white foam of the surf. He admired the way her bottom sat in the saddle. She'd gained more confidence.

At the *chop chop* sound of a helicopter, Massimo stopped Forza midstride and whipped out his phone. "Nicolo, are we expecting anyone today?" His full mouth thinned into a grim line. "Oh really? Summon her to my office at once."

"Is everything all right?" Emma asked, her voice full of concern.

"Nothing for you to worry yourself about. My mother invited Luisa."

Emma gasped. "No! I thought you said your mother was going back to Santino. If she isn't going, and now, Luisa is here, it is definitely time for me to go home. You promised... you wouldn't hold me here against my will."

Massimo turned in his saddle. "They will both be returning to Santino today. It is you I want with me, not Luisa."

Emma's eyes rounded, and she groaned, "Well, this is messy."

"Not for long," he said, pulling on the reins to turn Forza around. He wanted to gallop back to the stables but proceeded slowly so Emma could keep up.

They rode back through the surf and gave the horses to

the grooms. Massimo led Emma along the path through the garden and back into the castle. They took the elevator to the third floor and strode down the center of the wide marble hall to their apartment.

Once the footman closed the door, she said, "I'll stay in my room until they leave."

"No, Emma. You will not hide. Tonight, dinner, just you and me, the same as last night."

"What will your mother think? Shouldn't you have dinner with them?"

"I don't care." His arm curled around her shoulders. "And besides, they will both be gone well before this evening."

Emma sighed. "I have to get away from all of this."

He tugged her to him. "Good idea. We can take Steven to the beach."

"That's not what I meant—"

"It's a good idea, nonetheless. I have to go and talk with my mother. Lay down the law, as you Americans would say. Then, we can go to the beach. We can have a picnic."

"Massimo—"

His arms tightened around her. "Kiss me."

She groaned.

"Come on, you know you want to, and I really need to feel your lips on mine." He stroked her soft cheek.

Emma's arms went around his neck, and he felt her fingers in his hair. She parted her peach-tinted lips and did as he craved—kissed him.

"Say yes," he whispered against her lips.

She muttered, "Why do I give in?"

"Because you know the beach will be fun. Go and relax while I have a chat with my mother."

He tucked a tendril of red hair behind her ear and kissed the tip of her nose before he left.

CHAPTER 17

*E*mma walked into the half-lit nursery to check on Steven. He was sleeping in his crib with the nanny sitting beside him. "I'm going to take him to the beach later today."

"Yes, Miss Harris. I will have him ready."

Emma went back into her room to change out of her riding outfit. She chose a casual light-blue day dress and a pair of strappy open-toe sandals. Pouring herself a glass of ice water and grabbing her book, she headed to the terrace. A knock at her sitting-room door stopped her. She opened it, expecting to see the queen, but instead a tall, willowy blonde, perhaps twenty-five years old, greeted her. The woman wore a red boat-neck fitted dress with sleeves that ended below her elbows.

"Miss Harris," she said with a thick Malagran accent as she arrogantly strutted into the room. Her designer stilettos clicked on the marble floor as she made her way to the couch and sat down. "I am Lady Luisa Cristina di Molina, His Majesty's fiancée. I wanted to meet you privately so that we can discuss the nasty rumors that are buzzing around the kingdom." The woman pointed a finger at Emma. The long, red, manicured nail reminded Emma of a talon. "You have a baby who you claim is the king's son." She rested her hands on her lap, crossing her legs at the ankles. "Many royals throughout the world have illegitimate children. It is most definitely a part of life. I want you to know that your son will never be king. My children will be Massimo's heirs and not your half-breed."

"I don't know who you think you are coming into my rooms and calling my son a half-breed. No one calls him that."

Luisa pursed her lips. "You should leave now before word gets out. The people of Malagra won't tolerate an American with an illegitimate baby. Neither of you are welcome in Malagra. Once Massimo and I are married, I will be sure to ban you from the kingdom."

Working to contain her fury, Emma pointedly stared at Luisa's ringless fingers until the woman shifted in her seat and covered her left hand. "You don't know what you're talking about. Massimo, your fiancée, brought me here. Perhaps you should take that up with him."

"You know at all times, a commoner as yourself must address the king as His Majesty and never so informally." Lady Luisa stood and squared her shoulders. She lifted her chin higher and said, "I am the future queen of Malagra. You and your brat need to go." She lowered her voice as if they were confidants and said, "Miss Harris, men are men, whether kings or commoners, and I realize Massimo is having what I will categorize as a last fling with you before we marry. That is all this is—nothing more. Take your son and leave Malagra, now." Lady Luisa turned and strutted from the sitting room.

~

MASSIMO WALKED down the hall toward Emma's room. He'd just spent a trying two hours with his mother. She was determined to have him marry Luisa sooner than the planned August wedding date. She'd said he needed to forget about any fantasy of making his commoner paramour's son his heir. How could he even consider such an outlandish scenario?

That made him more furious than he'd thought possible. His mother's words echoed in his mind. "Marry Luisa, have legitimate heirs with her, and you can keep your lover on the side. You are entitled to that much. Malagra needs you, and you need Luisa. She is here and ready to—"

"Enough," he'd shouted. He couldn't think about his mother's demands. Finally, he'd ordered her to remove herself from his presence before he had his guards escort her from the castle. She stood and bowed to his wishes. "I want you to return to Santino now and take Luisa with you." He'd told Nicolo to see that they left immediately.

Massimo entered Emma's rooms through the bedroom and couldn't help but notice her suitcase beside the bed. Emma wore one of her dresses, not a bathing suit. "What is this?" He frowned at her.

"My clothes and Steven's. The ones we came with, nothing more. I expect you to honor your word—I want to go home, this very minute."

Massimo stepped over to Emma but stopped when she moved away from him. "We have another three days. And I will have them."

"You promised me. I want to take Steven and go home. I will not stay one second longer. Your fiancée explained everything to me, Your Majesty." Her voice caught on a sob. "How my son is a half-breed—"

He stormed over to her. "Luisa came here, to your rooms? When?"

"Don't be so shocked. After all, as she so kindly informed me, she is your fiancée and the future Queen of Malagra. I'm insignificant, just a, a… last fling before you and she marry. She can overlook that because men will be men." Emma balled her fists, resting them on her hips. She shouted, "The problem is that I can't overlook it." She gritted her teeth before she added, "You are keeping me here against my will. Pretending that we are—what I don't even know—and I have to find out that Luisa is still the one you will marry, and my son is considered a half-breed! Oh, it's all clear now. You are just using me to get to my son."

He grabbed her shoulders. "Do you hear yourself? What are you talking about?" he roared. "Luisa is out of the picture. You are the only one fretting about her. Why would you think that she and I hatched a plan to take Steven from you? And half-breed, what does that even mean? Is that another American idiom that I don't understand?"

"Don't touch me." Emma shoved his hands off her. She stepped a few feet away before she turned to face him. Emerald eyes blazing, she shouted, "Oh yes, Your Majesty, how silly of me to have to hear from that arrogant cow, Luisa, that she will not tolerate this! Oh, and my half-breed son will never be accepted by your family and especially not by your people. Her children will be your rightful heirs, and I have to remember my place. Which is *not* here in Malagra. And above all else, I must always use the proper address when speaking to a member of the royal family."

His body tensed. "Did Luisa say this to you? Why didn't you tell me—"

"I'm telling you now. You think I was going to come running to your office?" Emma stamped her foot. "I want to go home." Her green eyes glistened with unshed tears. Her chest rose and fell with her breaths. "I want to take my son and go home. You will not force me to stay here one moment longer." Her voice quivered.

He watched a tear roll down her cheek, then another before she swiped at her face.

His anger dissolved. Massimo wanted to kiss the tears from her wet cheeks. Take her in his arms and make everything better.

"I wish to add, Your Majesty, that up until you found out about Steven...well...until then... you had sent me home. You were continuing with your duty—to marry Luisa. In Rome, you didn't even tell me who you were."

"So, now I'm manipulative and deceitful. Is that what you are saying?"

"Yes," she sniffed. "That is exactly what I'm saying."

MASSIMO RAKED his long fingers through his raven hair. "There must be more to this." He pointed at the suitcase, nodding his head. "Luisa scared you off, I get it," he snickered.

"I'm a New Yorker. Believe me, I don't scare easily. Isn't it enough that she made me see how I don't belong here? I'm the other woman, and that is all I will ever be. Are you dense?"

"No one speaks to me that way. No one ever," he thundered.

The vibration of his voice went through Emma, dropping her own anger down a notch. "So, you don't have an answer, do you?" she needled.

Massimo turned to her, his body stiff, his fury visible in the redness of his cheeks under his olive complexion. "Is that what you think?" His nostrils flared. He lifted a black brow.

Emma couldn't turn away. She was mesmerized as he

took a breath and transformed back into the regal king he was at his core. He slid his phone from his pocket, pressed the screen, and said, "Nicolo, prepare my plane for immediate departure. Miss Harris is going home." He slipped his phone back into his pocket and said in just as calm a voice, "Remember this, Steven is my heir because I say so."

He turned on his heel and strode from the room.

CHAPTER 18

*E*mma's world shattered. This time she didn't crumble to the floor. Would Massimo try to keep Steven? How could she fight him? Emma ran to the nursery and threw open the door. Steven slept in his crib, covered in a blue blanket. His nanny looked up from her chair, eyes as wide as two saucers. Emma lifted a trembling finger to her lips, nodded, and slowly stepped out of the room. Her head pounded as she walked back to her sitting room. She slumped onto the couch as numbness set in. She didn't know how much time had gone by when Nicolo asked for entry.

"Everything is ready for you and the baby, Miss Harris. The nanny prepared a bag with his formula and other items you will need. She will accompany you to Brooklyn if you wish."

"No, that won't be necessary. I can manage on my own." Emma kept her voice flat, hiding the listlessness she felt. She vowed to herself not to ask where the king was, not with the way his eyes had pierced her before he'd walked out of her life. No anger, no emotion, only ice in the blue depths before he turned his back on her and sauntered from the room. *Did he even say goodbye to Steven?*

All his talk was meaningless. His unwavering honor and duty, along with the oath he'd made to his country, demanded that he marry a royal. That was all there was to it, end of the story. She couldn't stay in Malagra and be near him while he was married to Luisa. Now that she'd met his fiancée, the thought of Massimo and that blonde in bed together made Emma sick to her stomach. *I've been through worse... This is hopeless... He gave me what I wanted, to take Steven and go home, back to my life... So why do I feel so empty?*

Emma lifted Steven out of his crib and cuddled him to her, breathing in his baby-fresh scent. She wrapped his blanket around him, then hugged the nanny and thanked her for all she'd done. Nodding to Nicolo, Emma followed him out of the nine-hundred-year-old castle by the sparkling Mediterranean Sea to the waiting silver Rolls Royce. One of the king's royal guards stood at attention by the open back door.

Securing Steven in his car seat, Emma climbed in next to her baby. Keeping her eyes forward, she didn't dare turn to see if the king had come out to say goodbye. She couldn't shake the cold from her body or the hollow numbness from the pit of her stomach.

The plane ride and arriving home were all a blur. Emma had called her father once they were in the air and told him she would be home a few days sooner than planned. When Massimo's royal jet landed, a car waited on the tarmac to drive her home. With the time difference and the nine-hour flight, it was three in the morning before she climbed the steps of the brownstone. She would talk to her father in the morning.

Tomorrow, everything will look better. I'm strong and capable. I can put this all behind me. I will move forward. What was I thinking? That he would marry me?

Not happy with where her mind was going, she cleared the thoughts from her head.

Emma spent a restless night tossing and turning until she heard her father in the kitchen, making coffee. Steven's nanny wouldn't be back to work for several days, so she would take the remainder of her time off before returning to the office. The aroma of fresh-brewed coffee wafted through the air. She rose from her bed, put on a robe, and joined her dad at the breakfast nook. She was glad that he didn't ask her too many questions about Massimo and her time in Malagra. Once he left for work, she poured herself a second cup of coffee and sat at the table, watching the steam rise from the cup. She was too numb to do more. The dark and gloomy feelings from Malagra persisted. She didn't want to get dressed. Sitting at the table, she choked back a sob, thinking of Massimo. She folded her arms on the table and laid her head down, crying for what could never be.

Emma forced herself to care for Steven. She prepared his bottle, dragging herself to do what she had to. Take care of her son and most of all, forget Massimo. In the afternoon, she looked at herself in her ensuite mirror. Her face was swollen, and her hair hung in a straggly knotted mess. She wet a washcloth with ice-cold water and pressed it to her face.

When her father returned from work, she was still in her nightgown. "I picked up dinner from Nora's. I ordered your favorite, ravioli, and cannoli for dessert."

"Thanks, Dad." She grabbed plates and utensils from the cabinet to set the table.

"Do you want red or rosé?"

"The red for me," she said, while serving the food.

"How is Steven?" Her dad pulled the cork from the bottle of wine.

"He slept a lot today, but I don't think it's from the time difference. I bet he's going to have a growth spurt." Emma pushed her food around her plate, not really hungry. She didn't want to upset her father; she knew he had gone out of his way to order a favorite meal for her.

"How are you? Do you want to talk about… anything… the king, Malagra, the weather?"

Emma smiled. "You can always make me feel better, but it's so hopeless that I don't want to talk about him or anything else right now. I just want to—" She couldn't speak past the lump in her throat and turned from her father so that he wouldn't see her eyes well with tears.

"It's okay, sweetheart. You go rest. I'll load the dishwasher."

She nodded and hurried from the table, going to check on Steven before she went back to her room. She didn't want to read or watch a movie on the television. She didn't want to do anything but get in bed and pull the covers over her head. *Will the ache in my heart ever go away?*

Emma gave herself one more day to wallow in her depressed state before she forced herself to come to terms with the fact she would always grieve for a love that could never be, but she had to pick up the pieces of her life and move forward. If not for herself, then for Steven.

HER SECOND DAY back at work was King's Day in Malagra, Massimo's birthday. Emma couldn't help herself from checking it out. She closed the door to her office and sat behind her desk. She bit the corner of her lower lip as her finger hovered for a heartbeat before she pressed the trackpad on her laptop. She scanned the internet for news. A headline with color photos caught her attention. The lead picture was of Massimo, dashingly handsome in a dark-blue uniform with a red-and-gold sash anchored to one broad shoulder and across his chest, down to his narrow hips. The king stood on the grand balcony of the royal palace in Santino. The photographer had caught him looking up at the fireworks display. But the photo that really grabbed her attention was the one of him earlier in the day standing on that same balcony as a parade in his honor marched by.

Emma read the caption under the picture, naming Queen Gabriella and next to her Lady Luisa. On the other side was his sister Princess Elenora and his brothers Prince Gian Luca, Prince Enrico, and Prince Alfonso. Behind them, other family members stood. She recognized his cousin Prince Gino in the group.

Emma caught herself trying to enlarge the photo to see if Luisa wore a ring on her left hand. She gasped, disgusted with herself, and slammed her laptop closed. Lifting the receiver on her desk phone, she decided it was absolutely necessary to talk with Mr. Collins. She called his assistant and requested a meeting. Emma couldn't work on any projects involving Malagra or, for that matter, any of the surrounding countries. Would Mr. Collins figure out that there was a connection between her and the king? He was intelligent and might connect the dots. Her phone alerted her to an inter-office message. Mr. Collins could see her now.

She hurried to his office. Once she explained her situation, Mr. Collins agreed to assign her to a different project, and certainly nothing that would take her away from Steven for long periods of time.

Happy that she'd spoken with her boss, she went back to her office, making notes, tying up loose ends, and closing out all the files on the hospital project in Malagra. She was prepared to give everything over to another engineer.

Emma was elated that she could relinquish the liaison position and not have any contact with the Minister of Urban Development, Prince Gino, or anyone else in Malagra, especially the king. She would work with a different architect on a local airport extension project.

Ten days after King's Day in Malagra, meant two weeks since she'd returned home, and Emma still didn't know if Massimo had finally proposed to that horrendous woman.

Instead, she immersed herself in her work on the new project. Driving to the airport in Queens from her home in Brooklyn was better than taking the subway. It meant that she could be home quicker and spend more time with Steven She managed to share dinner with her dad most nights though she was too exhausted to do more than eat and take care of Steven. Her father didn't press her to discuss Massimo or her time in Malagra. One evening while they sat in the living room, Steven in his swing, her father asked, "How will the fact that his father is a king affect Steven when he grows up?"

She sighed. "Massimo is marrying someone else, and he will have legitimate heirs with her. Steven is *my* son, and... I can't think about Massimo. I know that when Steven is older, I will have to tell him something."

"I'm sure you will do what's best for you and Steven. You'll know what to say when the time is right."

"Dad, I would be content nurturing him with the same love and understanding that you raised me with after Mom passed."

"You are a strong and independent young woman, I'm proud of the person you've become."

"You taught me to think for myself and that is the best parenting gift you could have given me."

Another week went by, and Emma was getting better at keeping the sadness from showing on her face. One day while checking her emails on her lunch hour, she opened an invitation to attend a seminar in Rome on ancient Roman concrete. That night at dinner, she mentioned it to her father. He encouraged her to go.

"How could you not? It's a subject you're passionate about. I'll help the nanny take care of Steven."

The next day, she received an email from the company's in-house travel service. Emma scanned the itinerary with her flights, the seminar schedule, and the hotel reservation. "No, this can't be." She lifted her desk phone and called the travel agent. "Hello, Estelle. It's Emma Harris."

"Did you receive your itinerary?"

"Yes, but isn't there a different hotel I can stay at?"

"That's where we have our corporate account in Rome. I can check to see if there is another hotel, but the seminar is at the Grand Hotel Medici's convention center. Is there a problem?"

"No." Emma sighed. "I had hoped there were other accommodations. Thanks all the same."

EMMA USED TO LOVE ROME, but all of that changed after she met His Majesty, the King of Malagra.

Exiting her taxi, she stepped into the beautiful glass-and-mirror lobby of the Grand Hotel Medici. The lobby was busy at this time of day with guests checking in and others checking out. She stood in line until it was her turn, then she wheeled her suitcase over the granite and marble floor to the front desk.

"*Benvenuto,* welcome to the Medici. Do you have a reservation?" the clerk asked in his heavily accented voice.

"Yes, from my company Collins and Collins Architectural Design. I'm Emma Harris."

"May I see your documents?"

She handed over her passport. The clerk looked at the information, then handed it back to her.

Taking an envelope from the bank of cubbies behind him, he said, "Your room is ready. Will one key be sufficient?"

"Yes, that's all I need." Her name was printed in a fancy script on the front of the envelope. She opened the flap and glanced at the brass key. A memory assaulted her of Massimo using a brass key to access a private elevator at this very hotel. She snapped her head up. "This is wrong. This can't be the key to my room."

"Your company has paid for it. Is a suite not to your liking?"

"Don't you have anything else? I won't stay there," Emma managed through gritted teeth.

"Why on earth not? That suite is the finest accommodation we have. Top of the line." He lifted his hand, and a bellman in a teal uniform jacket with silver buttons, black pants, and black shoes hurried over.

Emma cut the bellman off. "I have one small suitcase and certainly don't need any assistance." She turned back to the front desk clerk. "There must be something else." *How could this be happening? Why that suite?* She clamped her jaw.

He stood there as stiff as the marble statues that were strategically placed around the lobby. "I'm sorry, Ms. Harris; we are full. There is no other available space."

She had a sense of déjà vu and closed her eyes for a second. She slapped her palm on the cold granite of the reception desk. "But—"

The clerk scowled at her, muttering something in Italian, then he smiled. "Madame, you are the first person in all my years at this hotel to become upset with an upgrade to the presidential suite."

Grabbing the handle of her carry-on, Emma turned and stormed from the lobby. She took several deep breaths as she wheeled her case toward the bank of private elevators and stood in front of a brass placard above the door with the words Presidential Suite written in a fancy scroll—the single elevator led directly into the living room of the luxurious suite. She knew what to do: insert the brass key into the keyhole and poof, the elevator doors silently parted.

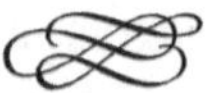

CHAPTER 19

*E*mma stepped onto the black granite tile floor and depressed the single button on the side panel. *Don't think, don't think, just breathe. You can do this.* She wouldn't look at the beautiful artwork hanging in the elevator or the tufted blue velvet bench against the back wall. She gripped the handle of her carry-on so tight, her hand hurt.

All too soon, the elevator door quietly slid open, and there *he* stood, tall and achingly handsome, impeccably dressed in a light-gray custom-made suit. "You did this?" She stalked into the living room.

A slow smile spread across Massimo's sculpted lips. "Red, what better place than where we met?" He took a step toward her, his muscular frame barely contained in the rich fabric of his double-breasted suit.

"Where you lied to me." She gave him a hostile glare.

"Never. I have never lied to you. I told you I couldn't give you tomorrow, and that I could only give you the time we had in Rome." His deep voice vibrated through her.

Emma fumed. "Where you hid your identity from me." She turned away from him, prepared to leave the suite. The curl of his long fingers on her arm stopped her. His body pressed against her back, and his warm breath on her ear held her in place.

"Where I fell in love with you, a woman who saw me as a man and nothing more," his tender voice whispered.

"Ohhh," she groaned. "We still can't be together—"

The scent of his spicy cologne drifted around her. His arms enveloped her against the hard frame of his body. His heat spread through the silk fabric of her blouse. Massimo held her against him, surrounding her as he leaned down, his lips touching her ear. "Now, I can give you tomorrow and all the remaining days of my life."

Emma tugged his arms from her waist and stepped away from him. Turning to face him, she stared into his eyes and demanded, "How can that be? What about Luisa? Your future queen," she sneered.

Massimo dragged her into the circle of his powerful arms.

"No." She pushed at the wall of his muscular chest. He dropped his arms, and she moved away from his towering height. "How do I address you? Is it Your Majesty or Massimo?"

"Call me Maxy... I love you, Emma. You are the one I want and need, the one I cannot live without," he said in his dreamy, accented voice.

She closed her eyes. *No, no, no. Why is he doing this to me?*

"Look at me." The rich timbre of his voice penetrated her brain. She opened her eyes to see Massimo bending on one knee. His long fingers opened the lid of a velvet ring box. "Will you marry me?"

She turned away. "This isn't funny. Massimo, you know that is impossible by your own country's laws. I can't believe your insensitivity at what you're doing."

Massimo stood, snapping the ring box closed before slipping it into his jacket pocket. "No Emma, you listen to me." He strode over to the sleek glass-top writing table in the suite. A crystal vase filled with two dozen long-stem pink roses stood to one side, and next to the vase was a red leather-bound folder.

Massimo lifted the folder, and Emma saw his royal crest emblazoned in gold. "This is what has taken so long."

"And what exactly is that?" She raised her hands to her hips. "It had better not be about my son."

Massimo's jaw popped once, and then the corners of his eyes crinkled as a slow smile spread across his beautiful lips.

So, I can't get him upset. Emma fought not to cross her arms over her chest.

Taking the steps to close the distance between them, he stopped in front of her. The top of her head reached his broad shoulders, and she had to stretch her neck to look into blue eyes rimmed with long, thick, black lashes.

"I must say that changes within the monarchy can be slow as it is steeped in protocol, traditions, and laws. It took more time than I would have liked to have The Succession to the Crown Act amended. The section declaring that the heir to the throne or king if unmarried must marry a person of royal blood has been deleted. The law that my great-great-great-grandfather added has been removed." Dipping his head, he leaned toward her. "I am free to marry you. The woman I love and no other."

Her tummy clenched. "Now. You choose now to do this? You did this without telling me?" She stamped her foot as anger consumed her. "All this time you have droned on and on about how you must follow the law. Your duty. Your honor. Your laws. Now all of a sudden, you're saying—" Emma snapped her fingers. "Just like that, it's all been changed. I find it difficult to understand. I can't believe that all along, you could have done this. Why didn't you tell me what you planned or, more so, what you were doing?" She moved away from Massimo. She shook her head and pointed to the leather-bound folder he held. "This is really about my son. You could have—" She stopped and took a deep breath. "I've told you Steven is not your heir. He is your illegitimate son—"

Massimo's deep voice oozed authority. "Yes, for now, you may think that... if you wish. That too has been rectified. The documents acknowledging Steven as my son were drawn up weeks ago by my lawyers. I have signed them. My last will and testament has been updated. And a decree presented to the prime minister has made it so." He caressed her cheek with his free hand. "I had to move quickly. Should anything happen to me, Steven will succeed me to the throne."

"I don't see how it's possible to change the fact that we had a three-day hookup in this very room, then after that, we went our separate ways." She shrugged. "I remember what you said. 'I can give you this time here and now. That is all I can share with you.' Those were your words. This is definitely about Steven."

"I remember telling you that you are the woman of my heart," he murmured, his voice tender.

Emma ignored the way he stroked her arm, sending tingles into her core. "Yes, you keep saying that. The part I can't understand is that you think I would allow you to steamroll me with pretty words. You think I would agree so you can take my son from me?" She turned away, unwilling to believe that he loved her and there was a chance for them. Her head snapped back. "What do you mean—should anything happen to you—how so?"

"My will has been changed to acknowledge Steven as my

son and my rightful heir. Anything can happen at any moment. It is my sworn duty as king of Malagra to ensure that the succession is secure. I have to be prepared for my country, my family, and you as well, Miss Harris." He placed the folio on the desk and walked to the window before he turned to her. The panoramic view of the city framed him as the sun played in his black hair, bringing out the blue highlights.

"Maxy… I… please no talk of dying. I know you don't want me. You only want Steven," she said, past the lump forming in her throat.

"What are you saying?" Massimo stormed across the room and dragged her in his arms. His powerfully built body enveloped her. His sapphire-blue eyes blazed. "I am not marrying anyone but you, so if you won't marry me, then so be it. I will never marry. Keep this in mind, Ms. Harris. Steven is my heir because I say so, and one day, he will be the King of Malagra."

Her peripheral vision dimmed. Emma's knees weakened, and he tightened his arms around her.

Her heart pounded. The lump in her throat felt like a hot boulder burning into her chest.

Massimo steadied her, slipping his hands to circle her waist. He searched her eyes.

"I can stand," she grumped.

"Good," he said, "So—"

"Wait, Massimo, please hear me out."

He nodded, taking her hand as they walked to the moss-green satin sofa and sat down.

Emma faced him. "Massimo, try as I may, I can't forget that until you found out about Steven, you had sent me home. You were marrying Luisa. That night we spent together in Santino, you said that you had to do what you must, and it was not a life with me. I can't get past that you sent me home and only after you found out about Steven—"

"You will not forget? You're saying that we don't have a future? I am truly sorry that I have made you feel that way. I never wanted to hurt you. That was never my intention. You are the only woman who has consumed my thoughts both day and night from the first day we met." Massimo kissed her hand. "My mother overstepped, going against my wishes. Luisa had no right to come to your room and say the things she said. Wait here." He stood up and stepped into the bedroom quickly, returning to sit next to her once more. He held a flat red velvet box in his hands. "For you." He opened the lid of the case for Emma. Her gaze caught his, and her eyes widened when she saw what was lying on the white satin interior.

"Emma, you are the woman of my heart. This belongs around your neck, always. I've had the diamonds added, so now, it is an exact replica of my signet ring. There's another touch." He pressed on the emblem in the center, and it opened.

"I didn't know it did that."

"The secret compartment has always been there. I asked the jeweler to set the three heart-shaped stones into the center. The ruby, emerald, and diamond to spell Red."

"I don't understand."

"Of course you do. I love you. You are the only woman I have ever given this medallion to. Emma Louise Harris, you are and always will be the woman of my heart. You are the only woman I have been with since the first time I held you in my arms. Emma, you are all I want and need. I will admit our son is the thread that binds us." He slipped the gold chain of the medallion over her head.

She gazed at him, her eyes narrowing. "How did you do this?"

He grinned. "I enlisted the aid of your father and your boss, Mr. Collins."

"My father helped you?" she asked, incredulous.

"Yes, we have become close while we video chatted and messaged—he's become proficient." Massimo turned her hand palm up, never taking his gaze from her. He brought her hand to his sculpted lips.

She couldn't turn away from him. His blue eyes compelled her to believe him. Massimo said, "So, do you want to marry me?"

Her breath hitched, and she whispered, "I want nothing more than to be your wife... But—"

He raised his hand to prevent her from speaking. "No buts. Say it again."

Emma frowned for a heartbeat before she said, "Yes, yes, yes, I will marry you, you stubborn man." She smiled at him, vigorously nodding, and she fell against his broad chest. She wrapped her arms around his powerful neck, arching her body into him. Massimo lifted her onto his lap and gave her a gentle kiss on her brow, dragging her firmly into the warmth of his body. He cradled her head in his hands. He kissed her eyes and the tip of her nose before he nipped her lower lip. She sighed in complete bliss. He traced her lower lip with his tongue. Emma parted her lips, melting into his hard frame.

One powerful arm came around her shoulders and his other around her waist as he crushed her to him. A wild swirl of desire set her on fire, and she gave herself freely to the passion of his kiss. She breathed in his scent. The taste of his tongue was familiar and welcoming. She'd feared to never be held in his arms again, and now, he was exploring her mouth as if this were the first time. His kisses slid along her jaw and down her neck. Her lips burned with desire.

Massimo removed the ring box from his pocket and

opened it again. "I could have picked an engagement ring from one of my ancestors, but I chose the stones and told the jeweler exactly what I wanted. Something that is as special as you." He slipped the emerald-cut diamond with heart-shaped ruby side stones onto the finger of her left hand.

"Massimo… it's beautiful."

"You are the beauty. Come with me." He led her from the living room to the bedroom. She smiled at the single pink long stem rose that rested on one pillow. His mouth was a sensuous caress as he bent to kiss her. Long lingering kisses that made her rise onto her toes to fit against his hard body. Next, his fingers lingered at her zipper. He kissed her neck while sliding the zipper further down her back. "Are we going to practice for our honeymoon right now?"

His lips against her throat he said, "I don't think you need to practice. How can you improve on perfection?"

"You are perfection. I love you, and I have missed you more than you could know. What about the rose?"

Massimo tugged her to him. "For later, right now I have other plans I hope you will like. I crave your taste on my tongue."

She swayed toward him and her core throbbed at his words. He slipped her dress over her head, dropping the comfy travel outfit to the carpet. He unfastened her bra before he slipped his hands to her hips pulling her against him. He nipped at her breasts, sucking a nipple into his hot mouth before moving to the other. He knelt, trailing kisses over her belly and down her abdomen.

"Maxy, I missed you so much." Her core flooded with flames of desire.

Emma stroked his head as he slipped her panties down her legs. He nuzzled the inside of her thigh kissing her. His finger stroked her, and Emma dug her fingers into his thick black hair. The thrust of his tongue replaced his finger. On the third thrust he stopped and swirled his tongue in her center.

"Ohhh, yes you're making me— she couldn't finish her sentence. She needed this more than she needed to breathe. He grabbed her butt, pulling her into his mouth. Licking and sucking her flesh, her clit was on fire. She tilted her hips opening herself fully to his magnificent mouth. She couldn't hold back the moan of need as pleasure pulsed through her veins. His tongue never stopped, and her clit became the center of her universe. Her hands gripped his shoulders as she writhed against his mouth. Quivering ripples turned into hot waves of pleasure as she came against his mouth.

"Please, take me to the bed," she panted barely able to stand with out him holding her up.

"Ah, Red, music to my ears." Massimo stood and lifted her into his powerful arms. "I have a better idea, one I think you will like." He carried her into the ensuite.

The only light was from dozens of candles flickering and casting a yellow glow around the sunken tub. Pink rose petals were scattered amongst the candles. A beautiful centerpiece of roses, long-stem, fully in bloom, to simple buds, had been arranged on the farthest side of the tub. Velvety rose petals led the way into the water, with some floating in the huge tub. "Oh, Maxy you remembered how I wanted to use this tub, and you've made it so romantic."

"I remember how we never made it past the shower."

She giggled. "Yes. Hurry and put me down, so that we can get you as naked as me."

His smile dazzled her as he helped her stand near the edge of the tub. She tugged his open shirt off while he dropped his pants and boxers in one move, kicking them out of the way. Emma descended the two steps into the warm water. Massimo grabbed the champagne and filled the two crystal flutes that were by the tub. He followed her into the bath, sitting on the tub seat next to her. "A toast to you, the woman of my heart." They touched glasses and drank before he bent to kiss her. "I don't want to wait to get married." Massimo's husky whisper sent heat through her body.

"Can the king of Malagra elope?"

"No, but we can be married in a month. Tomorrow, I can have your father and Steven fly to Santino. The prime minister will announce our engagement. You can fly to Milan or Paris to choose a wedding dress."

"Oh, what type of dress… I don't know the first thing about proper protocol or what I'm supposed to do."

"Red, you don't worry about that. Nicolo will have one of the palace stylists help you. I'm sure that my sister will be happy to advise you. Right now, you are sitting too far from me, I would prefer you come here." He lifted her by the waist, and she straddled him.

"I agree, this is much better." Emma took his hard shaft into her, happy to set the pace until she became frantic with need. Massimo placed his hands on her hips, lifting and lowering her on him until his breathing increased. His face, chiseled in stone, his muscles bulged as he dug his fingers into her, causing her to shudder with her own pleasure as Massimo erupted in her. Emma rested her forehead on Massimo's chin. "We made the water boil and the roses wilt," she said before kissing him.

"I'll buy you more. Let's see what we can do to the bed." He lifted her out of the tub to stand on the side, then grabbed two towels. They tenderly dried one another so they could do it again.

Hours later, Massimo reclined on his side of the huge bed facing her. "We are going to have the best life. You are going to make a great queen."

"All I want is to make you happy and for you to be proud of me. How will I know what to do?"

"You will be perfect."

THANK you for reading A Royal Romance. I hope you enjoyed Emma and Massimo's love story.

Have you read A Royal Temptation? That is the first book in my Royal Series.

ABOUT THE AUTHOR

USA TODAY Bestselling Author **Cindy Redding** writes what she loves. Contemporary, sizzling hot and spicy romance. Inspired by her travels around the world and her love of Italy, Cindy's romances come alive with hot-blooded heroes and strong-willed independent heroines. Escape to a world where happily ever after lives.

WHERE TO FIND MY BOOKS

You can find my books at your favorite bookstore, retailer, or library 

Or, you can buy them directly from me at my website https:// CindyReddingAuthor.com

Or,

Cindy's Store https://payhip.com/CindyRedding

If you prefer, please scan this QR Code with your phone

ACKNOWLEDGMENTS

I would like to thank Heather Starling for her ongoing content critiques and editing.

I owe a special thanks to the members of my critique group. Keith Howells, Rima Bardawell, and Hali Neal.

Thank you to Christopher Hawke of CommunityAuthors.com for your invaluable advice and encouragement. A very special thank you to Traci Hall also of Community Authors for your wonderful edits. You helped make my story shine.

Thank you to SJS Editorial Services as always for your quick and thorough edits.

Cover Design, by Jennifer Holt.